TIE DIED

Books by Kathryn Elizabeth Jones

A River of Stones
Parable Series
Conquering Your Goliaths: A Parable of the Five Stones
Conquering Your Goliaths: Guidebook
The Feast: A Parable of the Ring
The Gift: A Parable of the Key
Heaven 24/7
Living in the Light
with M. Celeste Martin
Marketing Your Book on a Budget
Susan Cramer Mysteries
Scrambled
Sunny Side-Up
Hard Boiled
Over Easy
Brianne James Mysteries
Tie Died
Buckled Inn

A Brianne James Mystery
Book 1

KATHRYN ELIZABETH JONES

Idea Creations Press
www.ideacreationspress.com

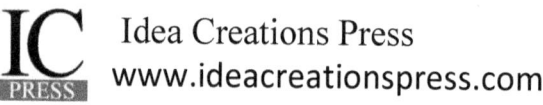

Idea Creations Press
www.ideacreationspress.com

This is a work of fiction. Any resemblance of characters to actual persons, living or dead, is purely coincidental.

978-0-9978-9046-4

Publisher's Catalog-In-Publishing Data

Name: Jones, Kathryn Elizabeth, author
Title: Tie Died / Kathryn Elizabeth Jones
Description: First trade paperback original edition. | Salt Lake City: Idea Creations Press, 2017.
Identifiers: ISBN 978-0-9978-9046-4 | LCCN 2017951358
Subjects: Mystery-Fiction. | Teen-Fiction. | BISAC: FICTION / Mystery & Detective / Amateur Sleuth

Printed in the U. S. A

Acknowledgments

A big thank you to my family who continues to support me on this writing journey, and to Lauren Holladay, my audio expert and new friend, who has brought all of my mysteries to life - including this one.

Frozen

I remember the day I found her. She was lying by the stream in Montgomery Park, where I always go when I'm out running, just lying there as if taking a nap. But it was November in Utah and it was odd that someone would be taking a nap in the snow. The water itself – was practically frozen, white glossiness covering most of the stream where I'd dipped my toes in just this past summer. The leaves were already gone from the trees and I felt suddenly as if I was somewhere I shouldn't be. My skin was cold and yet I didn't shiver as I looked down at the girl wearing the red running shoes.

She must have been running because she wore sweat pants – dark black with a white stripe down the legs, a tie dyed sweat shirt – and a scarf, still around her neck. It looked like wool. Her eyes were open – brown – and her hair, blond – no, more like a light brown with golden highlights. It lay crusted against the snow, glued to it almost; fanned out like the sun.

I didn't scream.

I reached for my cell phone in my back pocket and dialed the police, all the while watching the girl, her skin a light blue, her lips – white. How long had she been there? How had she been killed? Why had she been killed?

And then I looked at the bottom of her shoes. There was no mud. No snow. They were as clean as paper that hadn't been written on yet. The path was at least 20 feet from this frozen stream. She could never have jumped that far.

There were no tire tracks. Just one set of footprints coming to the stream and then away from it. They were large, much larger than her own and had diamond shapes on the bottom. . .

"Hello, Hello?"

"Oh, yes, sorry."

"Do you have something to report?"

"Yes. Yes. . . I found a girl at Montgomery Park. She's dead."

***

My mother is a worry-wart. Worse, she doesn't see that I'm old enough to make my own decisions. I'm old enough to go out running by myself at 6:30 a. m. before school, and I'm old enough to take care of myself.

But you know how mothers are; all ruthless and worrying, struggling to fix everyone's life without blinking an eyelid.

I sound cruel. I'm not. I love my mother, love that she took me and my brother, Oscar in – adopted us, grateful that we both have a safe house to live in and plenty of food and a place to sleep. And I'm grateful that there's more to life than searching for food when there's not enough – my past life – and keeping warm when there isn't a blanket and the heat is off – also my past life.

When I began running it was just a good way to find time for myself. I'm not overweight or anything, it was just nice to get out by myself for a while. Mom is always neck and neck next to me, and though Oscar couldn't care less since our move to Utah, Dad is getting sicker by the minute. I worry about him constantly, worry that he'll die and I'll be a sort of half-orphan all over again.

And so, I began running.

It started in the summer. Things were hot but if I got out early enough in the morning, before the kids came to the park and before the rays felt like melting magma, I could get in at least a half an hour or so before going back.

I could think about all sorts of things; boys, how I hated them, loved them. School; it sucked, it was cool. Friends; I hated, I loved them, and even my dad, though I tried to keep my thoughts brief where he was concerned, not because I didn't love him, not because I don't still, but because I would always have to stop and wipe my eyes so I could see in front of me.

Five months after beginning my running goal I was getting better. I could run almost an entire 45 minutes without getting so winded I felt as if I was going to pass out. Instead of returning home and lying in bed because everything hurt, I suddenly had more energy. Though my goal had never been to lose weight, you could say that my body was more toned than when I'd first begun, and I liked the way I looked in my clothes. That pooch of a stomach that had begun was becoming a distant memory.

The thought of my quickly fading stomach was the thought I had when I looked to the stream and saw the girl. It was almost ethereal at first, as if she was merely a vision or something, a beautiful addition to the quickly dying plants. But a person doesn't lie there, still, in the dead of winter, unless they're really – dead. And somehow, I knew the girl was dead even before I reached her.

Ever had that prickly thing on your arms when something is true?

Well, that's how it was for me when I saw the girl. I suppose I shouldn't be calling her that still. She has a name. Audrey. Audrey Wilkins. Sort of a prissy name if you ask me; the sort of name cheerleaders have, and beauty queens that get handouts all the day long.

Still, she was beautiful, even that day, with her frozen skin and frozen hair. She must have been there overnight at least or perhaps more than one night. How long did it take for the skin and lips to turn blue and waxy like those fake lips you get at Halloween, the hands to turn blue in the dead of winter? I looked at Audrey's head but could see no blood, though there was some dark liquid – almost black – pooled near her feet.

I looked it up, that day, after the ambulance arrived and took her away. After the police talked until I was blue in the face. Only then, near afternoon – I'd missed school because of it but didn't really care – did I have the time to look it up.

I had my own computer, though most of the students in my school did. Still, it was Oscar's old one, and that sucked. I planted the words, "How long does it take for a dead person to turn blue in winter?" hit the button and found this forensic site that told me some pretty cool stuff. Evidently, when a body has been lying around for about two hours, rigor mortis s them – making them as straight as a board – though not a very attractive one. As for the blue lips and white face, the stupid site said nothing; almost as if the internet folks were hiding stuff they really didn't want me to know.

But that was stupid and so I searched until I found it. The information was in this cool, *stages of death* chart. So, Audrey had been dead for about 30 minutes when I found her, so the killer may have been in the area when I was running the track, a true fact I didn't like.

What if he'd come for me?

I thought it was probably a *he* because of the big foot prints that went clear down the side of the path to the parking lot. When the cops arrived and after they'd asked me a million questions, including wanting my phone number in case they had anything else to ask me, I took off in the direction of the footprints as if I was going home, though home was the opposite direction. I followed those large prints all the way to the parking stall near the large oak. I studied the prints for a long time, placing my hands in my pockets for extra warmth, and then taking a picture of the large footprints with my phone camera. It was bright out so I took many pictures, hoping that one of them would turn out. The car was gone, but I took a few pictures of the tire treads too, hoping beyond hope that I could at least learn the make of the tires, connecting me with the sort of car the man had been driving. But even here I could see that the treads were slim; that whatever the killer had been driving, the car had been in need of a new set – they were practically bald.

Mom was already at work. She had her license now and worked with Dad at *Team Shadow Incorporated*, having finally sold her business to Jane Dove. The move had been scary for all of them, but they'd needed a new start. And besides, what better way to start a new business than in a new place where they could start fresh?

But in Utah?

I remember laughing at the thought of coming to Mormon town, but Mom wasn't laughing as we packed the last box and put it in the moving van. Oscar was furious. He hadn't yet started college, not really, unless you counted going for about two weeks and then dropping out because of boredom – as starting. He wanted to move out, but he'd had no job upon leaving our place and he had no job now.

I spent the rest of the afternoon to evening doing detective work on the internet, and had finally come to the conclusion that I would never figure out the tires, and I would never know about the shoes with the diamond soles the killer wore, when I found it. Because I'd also taken a photo of the girl's shoes and anything else I could think of to photograph surrounding her body; the trees leaning into the cold stream, their branches crusted and stiff, the water, still and frozen to the banks, even the girl before the police arrived. I had a slew of things I could check out, and wasn't afraid to do so.

No, I didn't do anything illegal in taking those pictures, at least not that I know of. I was at a public place, not on someone's private property, and anyway, I'd taken the photos before the police arrived so I felt pretty safe.

By the time dinner hit, Mom and Dad were returning home, though Oscar was someplace nameless. He went out a lot now, more so than he'd been out before, and a lot of the times he wasn't even home for dinner. I wondered if he was still into drugs – that had been part of the reason we moved – but I didn't dare ask him, when I saw him, that is.

"How was school?" Mom asked. Mom always had this way about her that made you cringe a bit. She could look deeply into your eyes, and almost read the thoughts written behind them. I could never lie to her and get away with it." I didn't go."

Of course, Dad wasn't like that. If wool could be pulled over his eyes, he'd be the first one to experience it. He peeked around the door.

"What have you been doing all day?" He smiled at me, walked in, and plunked himself on my bed.

The room hadn't yet been painted, but I'd purchased a new black and white comforter for the bed and the place looked great – considering.

"There was a dead girl at the park."

"Montgomery?" Dad asked.

"How did you guess?"

"It's the only one you run at as far as I know," Mom said, standing next to the computer and leaning in. "Are those pictures of the crime scene?"

I'd already downloaded them onto the computer, along with my notes about what I'd witnessed.

I nodded, turning back to watch Dad. He was grinning over at me. "And I suppose, you're going to solve this crime, if indeed there was one."

"What do you mean?"

"Maybe she committed suicide."

"Probably not." I pointed to the blood near Audrey's feet, to the pictures of the shoe prints walking away from the body.

"Okay, so what do you think happened?" Mom was curious now. I could feel her breath on my back like a wild animal puffing.

"I think she was killed somewhere else, taken in a car with bald tires to the park, lifted out of the back seat or the trunk by a large man, or at least a man large enough to carry a teenage body, and carried over to the stream at Montgomery Park where she was deposited."

"Why would someone do that?" Dad asked.

My skin prickled at his words." I think she was kidnapped and the kidnapper couldn't get anyone to give him the money he wanted," I said. "And the man, whoever he is, had to dispose of the body somewhere. It's cold out; probably thought he could do it without anyone seeing him."

"I see she is wearing a jogging outfit," Dad suggested.

"So that 'other' thing probably didn't happen," I said. I knew what I was thinking but I couldn't bring my mouth to say it. If the girl had been naked it would have meant something entirely different to my mind.

"Well. . ." Mom paused, took a deep breath, and placed her hand on my shoulder. "It might have happened earlier."

Darkness filled my soul.

"She didn't have any bruises that I could see," I said. "She was just white and blue and dead."

"I bet that scared you," Dad said.

"No. I was just curious about what had happened."

"You weren't even scared – a little bit?" Mom asked, removing her hand from my shoulder and squatting down near me. Her breath smelled suddenly of onions and I wondered if she and Dad had already had their dinner.

"Okay, maybe a little. It was creepy, but I was more interested than anything else. Do you know that it takes about 30 minutes after death for a corpse's skin to change color?"

"What do you think I do for a living?" Dad asked, walking to the other side of me.

"Oh, right. So, do you think I can solve it?" I asked, hoping against all hope that there wouldn't be any problems with doing my own detective work, that Mom would let go for more than a second, and that Dad would realize I was pretty serious about this.

As an 18-year-old senior I was finding it difficult to make new friends at the new school and it was just my luck to find something intriguing to take my mind off my sucky life. It was time for a change, and my first case was going to do it for me…

Thawed

Days later, I learned that Audrey's body had thawed long enough for the coroner and forensics to see some underlying clues that they'd missed on the first once-over.

I'd read about some of these clues on various online newspapers, others I'd managed to extricate from the lame cop who'd interviewed me once again two weeks later.

"Did you see the murder weapon?" Officer Hybrid had asked. I'd almost laughed looking at his name badge, but tried to remain calm. At the back of my mind I kept reminding myself that I would get more information from this cop if I wasn't giggling my way through it. Still, the man sort of looked like a Hybrid car. He was short, stout, and had large eyes much too large for his head. They blinked over at me like headlights.

"Nope. How bad was the stab?"

"Pretty bad; I mean, you didn't see the murder weapon then?"

"No, just the blood coming from her feet."

"I see." He wrote something down.

"Why was it purple? I mean, I thought blood ran red."

He touched his thick eyebrow. Funny gray hairs were sticking straight out and I wondered if he had to wet them in the morning.

"Blood always runs to the lowest part of the body. It's always that color."

"Even in the snow?"

"Especially then."

I'd already read about the body being moved from one location to another – and that the police were in deep 'do-do' because evidently the cop taking the call just two days prior to me finding her, had laughed off Audrey's worrisome concerns, telling her that there was nothing he could do about some strange hooded person following her; something about the Police Complaints Commission investigating the call that the officer had laughed off. I also learned that she'd more than likely been killed that morning at 6 a. m. She'd gone running right after breakfast, before school. Only she hadn't arrived.

"How far did Audrey live from the school?" I asked.

"Oh, about two blocks or so." The officer wrote something else down on the piece of paper.

"What was the knife like?"

"Did you see it?" Officer Hybrid asked again.

"No, of course not; just the blood, like I said."

"I can't give out that information."

"Why not?"

"It's part of the case –evidence. Did you see anything… unusual around the body?" he asked.

"No, not really; just lots of ice and snow. But the way the girl's hair was lying all around her – I find that strange, don't you?" I hoped the cop couldn't tell my heart was beating so hard and fast I wondered if it would burst from my body, but I had to ask the question. I had to know.

"Her hair was all around the snow, almost like the sun's rays. Why do you think he would have taken the time to do that?"

Office hybrid shrugged." I have no idea."

"I think it means something. So, you kill someone, carry her all the way to the park, lay her down on the snow and spread out her hair. And you make sure she is lying by the stream. What does it all mean?"

Officer Hybrid's large eyes blinked." I think we're finished here," he said.

I couldn't believe it. I couldn't believe *him*.

"What do you mean we're finished? I still have questions to ask!"

"Not on my watch. Who's asking the questions anyway?"

I am, I thought but didn't say.

***

It was weird not having Dad home like I was used to, but at least it made things easier when it came to cutting class. Mom would have had a royal FIT if she'd known, and so, for the next week or so I'd snuck out after roll call, gone home for what I needed – gloves, a scarf – whatever.

Most of my teachers took roll once we were in class, except Mr. Jepson, whose wandering eyes counted seats almost the entire time I was in class. But science was like that; lots of tables and weird smelling stuff and dead lizards. It was a class I had to take, and it didn't interest me much until we were going to dissect something.

It was cool looking inside an animal and seeing the guts. And while most of the other girls spent their time covering their eyes and holding their noses, I spent my time wisely looking over the interesting innards.

Conner Ryan, my science buddy, was *all that*. He wasn't too smart, but in looks, where it counted, I counted myself lucky to have him as a partner. He always smelled good; he probably shaved already, and his dark hair and eyes reminded me of chocolate.

We'd never kissed, but I wanted to in the worst way. So, we hadn't dated either.

Math was a different deal altogether. Mrs. Wang, of Chinese descent, was very smart. She'd write the problems on the dry erase board like a military pro. Some of it I understood, some I didn't. And she'd speak to us in broken English, most of which I didn't understand. I was getting a C in the class, but that wasn't from lack of trying. Most of the time her back was to us; I could leave her class – easy.

The same was true with my third class, English with Miss Meacham. I don't know what it was about her, but she could plant her head inside a book faster and for longer than I could focus on boys. Once the assignment was doled out – usually something cheesy like reading a chapter from the novel of the week, or figuring out some lame diagram for sentences, she would either fall asleep on her desk or take off for a few minutes to use the restroom.

I thought, being as young as she was, that she was either staying up all night with her boyfriend, pregnant, or both. She was nice though.

Two hours away from school, and right before lunch, made it easy for me to do some detective work. Lunch was roughly an hour, so I had three to do some sleuthing before returning after lunch to my art class – a class I never missed.

There was something about Mr. Cordial that a person just couldn't miss. He was like chocolate of a different kind. He was too old for me, I knew that, but I had secret hopes that perhaps he was the one staying up late with Miss Meacham, though I doubted it. Miss Meacham seemed about his age, and she had this wispy blonde hair and deep green eyes, which I figured most guys liked, even the older ones, but she didn't seem quite good enough for Mr. Cordial. Maybe it was because of her quiet way, her almost sedentary way of keeping her nose in a book that convinced me that the two of them would never make it as a couple. I just knew that if I'd been older, I would have asked him out.

He was standing before all of us now, like some sort of Greek god, and I couldn't help myself –
I laughed.

"And what do you have to share, Brianne?" he asked.

"I…I have my project almost finished." Actually, I hadn't even started it yet. It was supposed to be a self-portrait, one of those where you paint yourself instead of another subject, and I just hadn't been able to get my thoughts around it to begin.

"Good."

He turned to the class, and I drew in a quick breath. What would I have done if he'd asked me to show it to the class? But then, Mr. Cordial was cordial; he never did or said anything that wasn't nice. I smiled up at him.

"Your self-portraits are due next Monday, a week from today, so let's get going."

The class stood, almost simultaneously, and walked to their art bins. I stood and walked to the bin with the empty paper inside. On the corner, I'd already written my signature. I pulled out my paints and brush and reached for a cup closer to the sink.

"Almost done, huh?" Jordan said, nudging me.

"Shut up. The idea is in my head."

"He's going to find out, you know."

"So, what? Even if he does, he won't say anything. He never says anything about that sort of stuff."

Jordan grinned wickedly at me, as if he could see past my eyes to the back of my skull. His teeth were yellow, almost the color of bananas and his body smelled like wet socks. I tried not to breathe.

"Suit yourself."

He turned from me and reached for his own bin. I looked up at the front of the class. Mr. Cordial was already looking at me.

That day, before the art class, I'd managed to scrounge up some information on Audrey Wilkins. All it had taken was a short visit to the library, and an even shorter walk to the park where she'd been *planted*, more than likely having been killed before she reached the park.

After reading two newspapers, both local to Utah, I was also able to salvage bits and pieces from a national online magazine. Though nothing had yet been revealed about the type of knife used, there was plenty on the girl being taken by car to the park and disposed of. Nothing was said of the hair sort of flowing out like the sun, but there was plenty of information on the parents and what they were willing to do to find the killer.

Evidently, Audrey was their only child. She'd had a good life, enjoying anything outdoors including skiing, water skiing and snowboarding. She was a runner and spent much of her summers getting in shape for the next event, whether it was indoors or out. She loved to swim too.

Wow. I couldn't believe what I read. It was almost too good to be true. How could her parents afford all of Audrey's extracurricular activities? They must have had money, and tons of it.

I also couldn't believe that the girl got straight A's with all of these activities. She must have been way smart.

I left the library, pulling my coat tighter around me. That day I'd scavenged for some gloves, but I'd forgotten the boots, though the snow reached my ankles. Taking the pathways – some cleared, some not – I finally reached the park.

As before, the water was thick with ice, even thicker than it had been a few days past. I squatted near the banks and reached my finger towards the frozen water, stopping just in time as I wondered if my finger would stick. Looking up, I took notice of the large trees and the way the branches reached out its icy fingers to the sky. Walking to the area where Audrey had been *planted*, I walked through the short brush nearby, and, finding nothing but icy snow and dead branches, returned to the spot where I'd first seen her.

It hadn't snowed since her death, and the snow was packed tightly now where she had laid. The snow where the blood had reached had obviously been removed, and all I could see was the beginning of dying grass underneath. It was still green, though parts of it had begun to yellow. Kneeling down, I reached for a clump of snow closer to the tree. A great snowball, I thought, reaching out my hand and taking it in my palm. It was mostly ice, but something about it intrigued me. Though I hadn't noticed its presence before, the thing seemed already formed, as if someone, maybe even Audrey, had managed to pack the snow together before taking her last breath.

I looked down at it in my gloved hands and turned it around. A small spot of pink drew me closer. I thought of Audrey's hair like the sun, and suddenly, her tie-dyed shoelaces. Why was I thinking of that? Pushing my thumb into the hard crater, I pulled the snow away until it was revealed.

I don't know why I wasn't surprised, but I wasn't. It just seemed to fit.

It was a keychain – and not just any keychain, but a keychain of a sun.

***

"And where, pray tell, have you been?"

Prayer had nothing to do with my brother's late hour, or the fact that he was wearing a T-shirt and shorts in this terrible weather. But Mom, well, just think of it this way, her worry magnet was on again and she had no choice but to cling to it.

"Friends. Come on, Mom, I'm an adult." He brushed a fine line of snow from the top of his head, took off his shoes, and wandered into the kitchen.

Just as I had made my way back to the school, the snow had begun. I'd barely made it to art class before the bell had rung. Getting through the next few hours had been a real torture. I'd placed the keychain in my backpack, in the small pocket usually used for pens, and kept praying that even though it was zipped shut, I wouldn't lose it.

I finished the day with P. E., choir and history, and raced home, the questions of the sun keychain playing tricks on my brain. What did it mean exactly? That Audrey was still alive when she'd been *planted* at the park? It had to be. Why else would she leave a clue of a keychain nearby?

At dinner, I almost spoke up about what I'd found. Finding a note was one thing, but a keychain matching the dead girl's hair? That was just too weird to mention.

"So, how was school?" Mom asked.

"Good." I munched on a corn chip – tonight was Fritos night, a sort of Mexican concoction with chips on the bottom, layered hamburger, tomatoes, avocado's and cheese. It was Oscar's favorite. I just dealt with it.

"So, where were you?" My dad asked.

Dad was pale tonight, frozen pale.

"Out with friends."

Oscar sort of had this clamped-mouth way about him, especially lately. He hadn't been the same since the move, and I wasn't even sure if he had any friends. I wondered again if he was using drugs.

"Just friends. Really, Mom."

"Well," Mom answered just as smartly, "I need to know who they are. I need know *where* you are."

Oscar blinked over at me. It was strange.

"Well?"

I took another bite of chip and tried not to look at any of them. I didn't know who Oscar's new friends were. I hadn't seen him all that much. We were no longer together in any way, shape, or form and I had no idea what he was doing with his new life. School kept me pretty busy, and with the latest news of Audrey's death, it was all I could do to keep my own life going. Still, I felt sorry for my brother. I felt bad that he hadn't adjusted, if that was the word. I felt sorry that my parents had to harp on him. But most of all, I was sorry that he didn't seem to care anymore.

"I was at the movies, okay?"

"With who?"

"The guys."

"Names?"

"You don't know them."

I remembered the secrets in the past that Oscar had kept from Mom and Dad and hoped, no prayed – that he wasn't into drugs again, or drinking. I watched his eyes, but they didn't appear glazed. He wasn't smelling weird or anything like that. Still, it had to be something.

I stared over at him.

"What?!"

"I would like to know, too," I said.

"See, even your sister wants to know where you've been keeping yourself."

Dad took a bite, still looking pale. He had lost a lot of weight since the heart operation, and wasn't eating like he used to. Still, he was working at *Team Shadow Incorporated*, so he must have been feeling well enough to work. I loved my dad, didn't tell him often, but I loved him.

"Jeremy. Chad. Fair enough?"

"Last names please."

"I don't know their last names. Well, except for Chad's, but what does that matter?"

"Where do they live? Do you have their phone numbers?"

Oscar stood. He was 21 after all, old enough to be on his own. He hadn't made it through college, wasn't working, and had this secretive life. Still, it would have been nice for him to share – something.

"I'm going to my room."

I looked over at Oscar's plate. It was almost empty anyway.

"And your day?" Dad asked, fake grinning over at me. I knew he was mad, maybe even madder than Mom, though he rarely showed it. For Mom, it was all about firm control; for Dad, more like letting it fly, but I loved him too.

I grinned over at him. "School. You know."

I looked over at Mom. "Actually, we're doing these portraits of ourselves, which is pretty fun."

"Wow. What medium are you using?" Mom asked, taking a bite of her meal that hadn't been touched until now.

"Charcoal."

"That's interesting." Dad smoothed a hand through his hair and grinned over at me. The smile was a bit more believable this time.

"I guess. I like art. It's pretty fun."

"And your other classes?" Mom asked. I wanted to talk to them both about Conner Ryan from Science class but I just couldn't bring myself to do it. Instead I said, "Lunch is okay. And choir."

Dad laughed. "What a mix," he said.

I smiled and took another bite.

"You're not spending too much time on the Audrey Wilkin's case," he said. Dad sat up straighter in his chair." I read in the paper that the girl was out jogging when it happened."

"She was running before school," I said, as if he wouldn't have known that too. But the air was a little stagnant; I needed to keep the conversation going, at least for the sake of it turning back to me.

"So, what have you found out?" Dad asked.

"Oh, pretty much nothing."

29

Mom's eyebrows lifted. "Really?" she asked.

My heart thundered inside my chest but I tried to speak calmly. "I mean, she's 15, was running, and was carried from an unknown car and left for dead near the stream."

"There was something about her being stabbed."

"That, too." I tried to recall the feeling I'd had when it became clear that Audrey hadn't died until after she'd been carried from the car, that I knew it because of the keychain; because of the hair like the sun's rays against the firm snow…

"Are you okay?" Mom placed a thin hand on my forehead.

"Sure…sure. I'm just tired I think."

"Finish up and help me with the dishes. Maybe it wouldn't be such a bad idea for you to get some extra sleep tonight."

Weird Science

Conner smelled of shaving cream and his hair was combed back in that way I liked it – I could still see the comb strokes.

A small shudder caressed my back and traveled to my neck where it stopped. I took the dead frog and forceps and made a small cut between the hind legs. Taking the scissors, I cut the frog the rest of the way up, slicing the dead creature from bottom to top.

"I can't believe you can do that without throwing up," Conner said, taking the tweezers and opening the stomach to reveal the frog's innards. Mr. Frog was already pinned to the tray.

"Now," said Mr. Jepson, walking as he spoke, "I want you to label the parts. You should see the lungs, the spleen, and the large intestines. Extra credit will be given for labeling mesentery and oviducts. From the explanations to your left, you should be able to label all of the parts properly."

Conner leaned in. I could still smell him though the scent of formaldehyde was strong. "What say you give this frog a kiss? Wake him up."

"What?!"

"Kiss the frog. Come on, I know you can do it."

I couldn't believe it. I couldn't believe my heart was beating so fast.

I leaned in closer to Conner. "How about I kiss – you?" I asked.

If a thunderbolt had landed smack dab in the spot where we were working, the shock to Conner couldn't have been greater. He sat up straight in front of me, and, forgetting the tweezers, they clunked to the silver tray. He blushed. I had never seen Conner blush before. I didn't even know he could blush.

"Me?"

"Why, sure. Maybe you'll turn into a frog."

"Brianne? Conner?"

I looked to the front of the class. Mr. Jepson was staring over at us.

"Sorry."

"Do you have everything labeled?" he asked.

"Almost," I lied. I hadn't written a single word and neither had Conner. But he was no longer blushing. He picked up the paper and wrote some things down. Pushing the paper in my direction he asked, "Is this right?"

I looked at it. "You have the heart and lungs mixed up," I said. "I'll fix it."

It seemed as if time stopped as I wrote. I could still smell the shaving cream, still envision Conner's brown eyes on me; still see his hair falling into his eyes as he'd leaned in to ask me about kissing. But why had he asked me about kissing? Why, of all things?

***

It was night before I dared take the keychain out of my dresser drawer which I'd removed from my backpack. I'd looked at it off and on when I was alone, but I dared not keep it out for an extended period of time. And it wasn't just Mom I was worried about, it was everyone – Dad, Oscar, someone visiting – maybe even Grandma, though I hadn't seen my grandmother in months.

The sun itself was about the size of a quarter, the rays extending about a quarter of an inch beyond that. In the center, where a yellow stone might be expected – or at least a smiley face – was a blue stone. The keychain itself was made of bronze, and looked fairly expensive – maybe even handmade. It wasn't cheaply made, that was for sure, and as I looked down on it, my bedroom light off, my covers held high, a flashlight nearby, I couldn't help but admire it.

For a fifteen-year-old, this was some sort of keychain. Even the sun's rays were of different lengths. The strangest thing about this keychain, if you could call it strange, was what was missing: A Key. Who would carry a keychain without a key?

I thought of all the reasons why someone would carry a keychain without a key, and the list was short. The girl had had it on her backpack or purse for decoration. She'd lost the key or it wasn't her key-chain, but someone else's.

The last thought struck me as intriguing; I couldn't get it out of my mind, especially after turning the sun around and looking at what was engraved on the back: "I am not a morning person."

I'd missed it on the first and even second glance, but there it was around the back edges of the sun's center: *I am not a morning person.*

But Audrey was a morning person. That's when she ran. Still, it was obvious that her parents had money from what I'd read in the newspaper, so maybe the girl had been given the sun keychain as a gift. But why the strange message and why wasn't there a key attached?

I mulled over what the girl had been wearing – red Kobear brand shoes, dark black sweat pants with white stripes, a tie dyed sweat shirt the colors of the rainbow, a red scarf, more than likely made of wool… Why had I thought wool? Who would wear a wool scarf around their neck while jogging? Well, some people would, I figured. They wouldn't want to get cold, but if she was jogging, wouldn't she have taken the scarf off, and why around the head? To protect the sweat from dripping into her eyes, or something?

I thought then about all of the places a person could buy a keychain like this; online for sure. And then there were those specialty shops – card shops. Where else? Well, maybe she had purchased the thing for herself and had it engraved. No, she wouldn't do that, would she? Wasn't it more likely that someone had given her the keychain as a gift? Someone besides her parents? Still, if that was the case, whoever the gift giver was, they must not have known Audrey very well.

Would a fifteen-year-old girl have a boyfriend? Audrey had been in the 9th grade, and that meant the oldest age in middle-school. She would be thinking about high school, and maybe dreaming about her sophomore year. What if she had a boyfriend who was already in high school?

How large would the boy need to be to carry her all the way from the parking lot to the frozen stream? It was at least a two-minute walk. The boy would have to be large enough to carry her that far. And why – there? I'd noticed footprints, and fairly large ones, in the snow leading up to the stream. But what size? I'd taken a picture but I hadn't thought to measure them. Still, I had the diamond imprint of the shoes and that had to direct me somewhere.

Scrambling from my bed I scrounged through the top drawer to find the photo. With the flashlight, I peered down at the impression. There wasn't much there, just small little squares. What shoe had small squares on the bottom?

I brushed my fingers against my eyes and checked the clock. 1 a. m., placing the picture I'd downloaded and printed off of my computer into my purse, I clasped it.

Sun Stroke

The following day as I sat in history, dreaming of being somewhere else, maybe somewhere else in time, it occurred to me how big time was in this mystery.

A person didn't just get killed for no reason. They wouldn't be left in a park by a stream for no reason. Time and place was everything – often premeditated. Why the stream? Why was the killer wearing running shoes?

Okay, I didn't know for sure that they were running shoes. They might have been work out shoes or just 'let's put these shoes on and go kill a girl' type of shoes, but there had to be a reason the killer put these on versus dress shoes. I could rule out that the man was going to a party, or to church, though the day was wrong for that activity, not to mention the weirdness of a killer going to church in the first place. . . He hadn't been on his way to work, so that left a sport of some kind. A not-so-casual walk in the park. He wore the sort of shoes that could assist him in carrying a dead girl from the car all the way to a frozen stream without dropping her.

How much had she weighed? Now, there was a question. Could a deep or shallow indentation in the snow tell me anything about how much the killer weighed?

"Brianne?"

There was laughter in the room the size of a tornado. It spurted and whizzed from every corner of the room.

"Yes?" I tried not to hunch down, but the laugher was embarrassing. How long had Mr. Donner been speaking to me? And what was he saying now?

"Your answer?"

"About what?"

More laughter. I didn't dare look back. A creepy girl by the name of Janine Wilks was cackling like a witch. Her sour and high-pitched laugh made the hairs on my arms stand up.

"What was the question?"

Redness crept up my cheeks, but I tried to ignore it.

"President Abraham Lincoln. What strikes you as prominent?"

I couldn't help it; my mind was blank. "His nose?" I said.

The class wailed.

"About his presidency."

"Oh. He was a great president."

Janine poked my back. "I don't believe you," she said, her rancid breath reaching out for my neck and choking it.

I coughed. "And... I like and sort of hate how he felt about the slaves."

"Now, there's something. How did Lincoln feel about slavery?"

Silence filled the room. This is what was called a probing question, the sort of questions I'd tried to ask that stupid 'car' of a cop. And now the questions were coming back to haunt me.

"He hated it. He said that no one should own another human being. But he did feel as if the whites were superior. He didn't think we would ever be able to live equally with the blacks. Well, at least at first."

"And your view?"

"I think we're doing better, don't you?"

"In what way?" Mr. Donner was pacing now. His hand was under his chin. He appeared deep in thought. I couldn't help it. He reminded me in that moment of the statue of Abraham Lincoln in Washington D. C., all stone and seriousness.

"Well, even Lincoln's heart softened through time. That's why he supported black suffrage," I said.

"Good point."

Mr. Donner looked up "Any additional comments?" he asked.

The bell sounded and made me jump. I looked at the clock. It was 2:30 and school was over. This detective work was having its way with my brain. And this 'way' was not just occurring in class. It happened at dinner that night and the following morning as I was getting ready for school.

President Abraham Lincoln and his killer, John Wilkes Booth, must have been having a time of it in heaven – if, in fact, that's where Booth was – though I had a sneaking suspicion that he had to have been carousing somewhere else. Would God let a man like that into heaven?

***

"So?" Mom asked.

"So, what?" I answered, grabbing my backpack.

"After school. Want to go shopping?"

I thought about the run I'd miss once again for obvious reasons. Though I'd decided on running in the afternoons since the day I'd found Audrey lying by that stream, I hadn't managed to make the time.

I pulled the straps over my arms and reached for the door knob. Dad was still asleep and Oscar was who-knows-where, but it was nice to have Mom see me off.

"Sure," I said, hoping against all hope that I might discover the location where the shoes, the shoelaces, and the keychain had been purchased.

***

Mom was having a hissy fit but I just had to check *The Jailer*. I couldn't help it anyway; it was one of those weird stores in the mall that had everything a person had never even thought about owning; socks with toes, nail polish that glowed in the dark, even hair accessories that told you your mood – well, today I was happy and wanted to go in.

Mom peered inside. The window display was a menagerie of lip gloss, strange outdoor wear, and something that looking like a Slinky.

Mom held her nose as we walked in. "What is that stuff?" she asked.

"Can I help you?" a teenager asked from behind the register. I tried not to stare. Still, he looked kind of cool in a strange way.

"Yes, I'm looking for a keychain with a sun on it."

"Pinked striped or the prickly variety?" He spun the display around revealing three choices. Not one of them matched the keychain I had recently hidden inside my purse.

"No, this one is more real than fake – "

"Wouldn't be this store then, try *Clarities*."

"Where's that?"

"Just up the mall a bit. When you get past the creamery turn left. It's the second entrance on the left."

"Thanks!" I looked up at Mom. She was still holding her nose. I was so embarrassed, but figured not letting my unease show was the best solution. I turned from Mom and walked out of *The Jailer*, listening as Mom caught up from behind me.

"That place was nasty!"

"You should see *The Crawl*," I said.

Mom said nothing. She caught up with me and we discussed the case as if we were merely trying to decide what to cook for dinner. Mom was weird too, but she did understand a murder and all of the intricacies that went with it.

"So, why do you need a keychain?" she asked first.

"My old one is getting old."

"Why a sun?"

I shrugged my shoulders trying to appear nonchalant. "Just sounded good."

"Ok. So, what have you heard lately about that Wilkins girl?"

"Not much," I lied, "but I wonder why she was dressed as she was. Have you thought about that?"

"A little. She was into sports, right?"

"Right. But why the multi-colored outfit? Did she want to stick out or something?" I couldn't help it. I thought about the teen's hair behind the counter at *The Jailer* and the way his face had been painted. Perhaps it didn't matter that Audrey's shoes had been red and that she wore black sweats and a tie-dyed shirt with matching laces. But it just seemed a bit weird to me.

"There was a girl I knew when I was much younger," Mom began as we rounded the corner. "She mixed patterns and colors and weird styles but people still thought she looked pretty cute and tried to dress like her."

"Really? What was her name?"

"Punky Brewster."

"Strange name."

"Well, she was actually a television star."

"Oh." We stood at the entrance. It glittered and made my eyes hurt. *So much glitter, so little time*, I thought as we entered. The place smelled like roses with just a smidgen of antiseptic; *perfume, or something else?* I thought as I perused the aisles.

Most of the stuff I spotted would have made even a good flower wither, but this stuff was actually more in line with the sun keychain. There were regular jeans and T-shirts with pretty normal stuff on them; jackets and shoes; even shoelaces. Nothing tie-dyed though, and nothing that even closely resembled Audrey's keychain.

"This is all you have?" I asked the clerk. She blinked down at me and smiled. "Almost. We have some discontinued stuff in the back if you want to look there."

I smiled, trying not to listen too hard to the music playing over the sound system. Was that Elton John? I had heard Crocodile Rock more times that I wanted to count, though Mom was obviously loving it. I could hear her singing the words, feel her breath on my back as I walked to the back of the store and checked out the bins.

"Still wanting that sun keychain?" she asked.

I nodded, rummaging through the stuff.

"Well, here's a necklace," she said, lifting up a small sun on an equally small chain.

"That's nice," I said.

Mom leaned down again and returned to her own rummaging. The noise in *Clarities* had suddenly grown and I looked away to see who had entered.

"Don't say anything," I said, when I saw him.

"About what?"

I looked down at the bins, still rummaging but not really paying attention to what I was doing. "Nothing."

Mom looked up. "You mean those two? Hey, the boy's kind of cute."

My legs were shaking and I tried to think of something else. Why would Conner Ryan be in this girl store? And who was that with him? He didn't have a girlfriend, did he? I couldn't believe it. All this time, and he had a girlfriend!

I looked up to see him smiling over at me. He winked.

"Mom, we've got to get out of here," I said, trying to move past her and out the way we'd come in, but she'd already stopped me with her hand.

"Wait. Do you want me to say something?"

"No!" I hissed.

"What about the keychain?" She was suddenly lifting one up. I turned to glare at her but my heart stopped me.

"Where – Shhh! don't look over there."

"Where?"

"There." I pointed with my elbow.

Mom smiled, looking in the direction I'd told her specifically not to look. "Come on. Go over and talk to him. I'll even buy you the keychain." She dangled it like a dead thing from her pinky finger.

"I don't want it."

It was amazing, truly amazing. I was solid cement as I stood there. Time stopped. As my mother gaped at me and my skin flushed (it must have, I could feel it creeping up my cheeks), Conner approached. "Hey, meet my twin," he said, punching me in the arm.

I reached for the sore muscle and tried to look up at him normally.

"Your sister?"

"Pleased to meet you," Mom said.

I had to sit down.

"Hi, I ah…"

"This must be your mom."

"Yes."

"Where did you get that?" Conner asked, looking at me strangely. His brown eyes looked intently at the keychain as if it was the most interesting thing he'd ever seen.

I tried to answer him without passing out. "Back there?" I pointed. The bin was just behind me.

"That close? So how are you doing?"

"Good."

"And the frogs, how are they?"

"I – "

"Sorry, that was rude. We are science buddies," Conner said, looking briefly at his sister and then at my mom. We did this experiment recently, and your daughter was a big help."

"She was?"

Mom looked suddenly surprised as if she thought I was too dumb or weak or something to be carving into a living thing, and then she laughed. Eyes, other than our own groups', turned in our direction.

"Well, we'd better go. Maybe we should get one of those cool keychains for your friend?" Conner turned back to his sister. "This is Emily," he said.

"Hi!"

Emily's dark hair was pulled back into a ponytail and she had dark green eyes the color of emeralds. She was smaller than her brother, and wore an impish grin as she looked over at me.

I reached out to shake her hand.

She laughed. "So, you're the one," she said.

My heart caught in my throat.

Conner coughed and dragged her to the keychains.

I looked over at Mom. She was grinning too.

"Well?" I said, fingering my coat as if it would give me some sort of answer for what had just occurred. What *had* just occurred?

"I think he likes you," Mom said, handing the keychain to the clerk. "And I think you like him. Am I right?"

I looked back at Conner and Emily. Neither one looked over at me as they rummaged through the discounted items.

"So, when did you get these keychains in?" I asked the clerk.

She blinked over at me. "I'm not sure. You'll have to ask the boss."

"Is she – he, here?"

"In the back; why do you need her?"

"How long has the keychain been on sale?"

"Oh, about two weeks now; you got the second to last one."

She placed the keychain in a small sack with the receipt and handed the bag to my mom. "Still want to meet the manager?" she asked.

Mom seemed uncomfortable. She squirmed at my side, leaning in a bit as if she wanted me to share with her what was up. But I couldn't tell her what was up, could I?

"That would be nice," I said, trying to avoid Mom's movements.

"Well, okay."

My arms felt cold suddenly underneath the winter coat. Mom was as silent as death, though I could still feel her breathing beside me.

47

When the woman entered the room from the back I couldn't have been more surprised. She was familiar to me, but not in the way that familiar usually came about. Her light brown hair fell straight, almost to her shoulders and her piercing brown eyes reminded me of someone. The eyes, they were the same shape, and bore the same intensity that must have been in Audrey Wilkins eyes just before she was murdered.

"Mrs. -- Wilkins?" I asked.

"Yes. And you are?"

"Brianne James."

She reached her hand across the counter.

I took it and shook her hand briefly.

"So, what brings you to *Clarities*?" she asked.

"Oh, I purchased a keychain."

"One of the new ones?"

"No, one from the back."

The woman smiled pleasantly, though suddenly her eyes dimmed in intensity. "OH, which one?"

"The sun one," I said evenly, though my heart was thundering.

Mrs. Wilkins paled. "OH."

"I was just wondering how long it's been on sale."

"Oh, about two weeks; why do you ask?"

"No reason really. What company is it with?"

"You mean the maker?" Her smile relaxed. "Were you hoping to buy more of the same?"

"Maybe," I lied.

"Well, this particular item was bought through, let me see, Stanford. Do you know them?"

"No, but thanks. Can I stop by their place?"

"I'm afraid not. Well, not unless you want to travel to Chicago. That's where they're made."

"Handmade?"

"Yes, how did you know?"

"Just wondering. Can they be engraved?"

Mrs. Wilkins blinked over at me. I thought I was going to pass out for sure. She didn't wear a mean face or anything but something about her look made me feel funny inside. It was if she held a secret, a secret she would never reveal even if faced with death.

"I'm sure they can. Why do you ask?"

Her eyes were vacant though she was still smiling. The intensity was gone, maybe never to return.

"No reason. Thanks for your help."

I tried to breathe evenly as we walked away, my thoughts on what I'd just learned and who I'd just met, but it was no use, by the time I'd reached the entrance, Conner and his sister were waiting for us.

Science Experiment

It didn't take me long to realize that my mom was right. Conner liked me, though why I just couldn't begin to imagine. He was popular, I was not. He was hot; I was more of a lukewarm variety. Still, though none of it made even an ounce of sense, I liked it.

The next week, when I returned to school and went into Mr. Jepson's science class, Conner was already there. His eyes were pinned on me like glue; hot glue.

I sat on the swivel chair and dared not look at him, at least not yet.

"So you know, that keychain is pretty cool. Thanks."

"You're welcome. So, your sister's friend liked it?"

"The party was great, I guess. But you know how it is, going to a party your parents expect you to attend."

"Yeah." I looked up.

He was smiling at me, really smiling – even his eyes were smiling. It was almost too much to take in – to believe. So, you know, I am normally not the shrieking type. Sure, I like girl stuff, even gross stuff, stuff that boys live for, but I've never been the sort of girl who gets all giggly and stuff. But now, now I was proving myself wrong. Was this only Conner Ryan or some famous rock star looking at me?

I took a breath and continued to look at him, saying nothing. My lips trembled like my mom's kitchen mixer, and I knew my legs would be able to tell Conner how I was really feeling before long.

"So, maybe a date is in order."

What was he doing, ordering a pizza?

"I mean, only if you want to. I've already called your mom."

"What?"

"I mean, so I know she's a cop and everything, and I didn't want to push any of her wrong buttons."

"Her – "

"Hear me out. I know all about you…"

Mr. Jepson began talking then. He was speaking about some forthcoming science project, but I couldn't focus on any of his words.

"…about your mom and dad. About the crimes you've solved. I think it's cool."

"So, you want to ask me out because I'm a crime fighter?"

"Yes – I mean, no, I mean you're nice and everything, and I've been wanting to – "

"Conner and Brianne? Do you still want to be science partners, or should I set you up with someone else?"

Painful laughter like hailstones fell throughout the room.

"Quiet class! … Well?"

Conner looked away from me and to the front of the class room. "We can be quiet Mr. Jepson," he said.

A small chill caressed my arms and was gone. So, he had saved me. He had saved us both.

***

By the time lunch arrived I was totally and completely hungry. And for the first time, Conner found me and plunked his tray next to mine. I don't know if I should tell you this but I felt like throwing up in just that minute, though there was nothing in my stomach yet.

It was like someone was playing ping pong in there, but I couldn't let Conner see it – I couldn't let any of them – see it.

"Hi!" I said, maybe too loudly.

"Can I sit by you?" Conner asked, though his tray was already there. It seemed funny, but maybe he was just trying to be polite.

"Sure."

He sat, and in that instant, I smelled his aftershave. It was minty and lovely. I tried not to swoon.

I didn't swoon anyway, had never swooned, but I wanted to in just that moment.

"So, how long have you been shaving?" I asked, taking a bite of what, I do not know.

The bench we were sitting on moved at that moment, but there was no laughter. Surprisingly, no one appeared to have heard me.

"I mean, how was the party?"

"Like I said, okay. And yes, I did shave before I went. My mom calls me the *beast*. I guess she was worried about me a couple of years ago when she started seeing growth on my chin. I don't know, maybe she thought I was turning into a werewolf or something, but I got a razor for Christmas. Ever since then, I've been *the beast*."

I took another bite of food, glad I had something to do with my mouth besides try to answer him. How could a person answer *that*?

"Don't feel bad," he continued, taking a bite of his own food. So, it was enchiladas." I mean, everyone thinks it, but no one dares ask me about it. I like that you can ask me."

Redness crept up my cheeks, I could feel it. I suddenly felt wonderful and strange all at the same time. I'd never had a boyfriend before, though I'd gone on a few dates, ones my mom would say were nothing to write home about. And I had agreed with her.

Until now. Things were entirely different and I had no idea what to do with myself. Jane Dove, Mom's friend from New Jersey, must have known the feeling, though she'd gone for years before someone had finally wanted her – and even then, it had been for all of the wrong reasons. I wondered suddenly what Jane would have been able to teach me.

Conner nudged me. "Tell me why you were asking that clerk so many questions?" he asked, taking another bite." I mean, you were standing there for at least five minutes; there was even a line forming."

"There was?"

"Yeah, the lady behind you looked as if she was going to lose her girdle."

"What?!" I choked.

"Yeah. Ten seconds longer and you might have been on the other side of the counter."

I smiled over at him. "You're kidding me."

"No. I'm dead serious! When you finally walked over I was relieved on so many levels."

"Your sister seems nice," I said, trying not to dwell on the 'levels' comment. I would lose my mind – maybe even my stomach – if I dwelt on it. Besides, I had to get through this lunch.

"And," he took another bite, "I just had to ask you out. I mean, I know I shocked you when I said it but I've wanted to ask you out since you moved here. I just couldn't get past the parents. I mean detectives and all that. Or, are they cops?"

"My dad was a cop, but he had to retire from that because of his heart. My mom is a detective – she actually has her license and all that, though when she started it was just hit and miss. Now they work together."

"Where at?"

"*Team Shadow Incorporated*."

"Cool. So, what have you found out?"

"About what?" My tray was suddenly clean of all enchilada evidence, though I hadn't remembered eating any of it. Conner's was the same. He turned to me now, his hand lying leisurely on my shoulder.

"You know – that dead girl. You have to be working on that."

"You mean Audrey Wilkins?"

"Sure. That was her mother, you know."

"I know. So?"

"So, you were trying to get some clues, right? What does the keychain have to do with it?"

I couldn't believe it, but then maybe then I could. It felt like a spark of the sun's rays had suddenly hit my shoulder, but not in a heavenly sort of way.

"Is that why you wanted to ask me out?"

Conner raised his hands in the air. "No."

I stood, picked up my tray and glared down at him. "You know what; I was crazy enough to think you really wanted to date me! Imagine that!"

"No, no! I mean, yes!" He stood, knocking a fork to the ground. It clattered and stopped. I didn't care if everyone stared. Not this time.

"So, why the sudden interest in the dead girl, then, huh?" My hands were on my hips. I knew I looked stupid and desperate and like one of those *valley girls* my mom had once talked to me about, but I didn't care.

"I like you that's why!"

Cheering echoed in the lunchroom, cheering so loud I almost dropped my lunch tray.

I stared at Conner, really stared at him. Was he serious? Had he actually just been interested in what I had to say? I gaped at him, the words frozen in my throat.

"Finally, I can speak," he said, taking me by the arm and leading me to the tray drop off. "So, do you want to go out with me, or not?"

I left the tray at the drop-off spot and continued walking. I was no longer mad, just utterly and completely embarrassed.

Conner stopped me with his hand. The sun's rays seemed to burn through his fingers and to my shoulder.

I blinked up into his brown eyes, wishing he would kiss me in just that moment. It was strange, really, we'd just had our first fight, and now I wanted to kiss him? But my heart was beating like a thousand drums and my breath was coming too quickly to be normal. And he was smiling at me. Was he leaning in? Would he kiss me right there in the hallway with everyone looking? I closed my eyes. I could feel his sweet breath on my cheeks. But there was nothing.

"Are you taking a nap?" he asked.

I opened my eyes. A small tear had gathered there and was suddenly falling down my left cheek.

"There you are. So, do you want to go out or not?"

***

I smelled him even before I saw him.

"You'd better leave Conner Ryan alone," Jordan said.

I was on my way to math class, and would only ditch the class when Mrs. Wang's tiny body was turned to face the whiteboard. She never took roll herself and I'd made a deal with the roll-taker, Carly, to keep her mouth shut for a few extra dollars a week. I shouldn't have done it, of course, but I just had to go on the prowl – I just had to find out who'd murdered Audrey Wilkins.

"Why?" I asked.

Jordan's yellow teeth smiled at me. "Because, I know how he is with girls', that's why."

"And that is?"

"You don't have to be rude. But you need to be careful with him if you ask me."

"Well, I didn't ask you."

"Right. Well, see ya."

Jordan turned. For a moment, I watched him, his strange comments making the hairs on my arms stand up, the same way they'd stood up when Janine had laughed in science class, but I tried to ignore the feeling.

Walking into class, still wondering why Jordan would care enough to speak to me, I nodded at Carly who already had the roll on her desk.

"Now, class," Mrs. Wang began, stroking the marker in her hand like a favorite pet. "Remember the test comes soon; very soon. Study is practical and important."

She turned from them and began to write something on the board. Evidently it was the date of the next test. The following Monday I would have to sit there for the entire hour.

As the lecture progressed, I took a quick look over at Carly. I currently owed her $10. I wasn't working or anything after school, though I had thought recently about getting a job at the mall. The money would have to come from my savings and I wasn't sure how many more weeks I could carry on the ruse with Mrs. Wang before I ran out of money.

This was the third time I'd ditched math class, and I also wondered how long it would take any member of the class to continue their silence. I hoped for another few weeks, but one could never be sure about something like this.

I stood quickly, trying not to knock the desk with my body, and retreated to the door near the back of the class where I'd managed to escape before. Fortunately, I had no enemies that I knew of in math class, and I was able to escape without a hitch. Except for one thing: Conner was waiting for me.

"I knew it," he began.

"Knew what?" I tried to offer nonchalantly, pulling my backpack over my shoulders and moving to the outside door.

"This escaping thing you've been doing."

"I'm not doing anything." The last thing I needed was someone tagging along. "Why aren't you in class?" I asked.

"I could ask you the same thing." Conner stopped me with his hand. The warmth burned.

"I… I have a pass."

"Let me see it."

"It's probably at the bottom of my backpack."

"I'll wait."

"Come on, Conner."

He led me to the doors. Pushing the first door open, we slipped through. As the first door swung closed, he pushed open the second, still holding my hand.

"Where's your coat?" he asked.

"In my backpack."

"Get it."

He released my hand and I pulled the backpack from off my back, unzipping the large opening.

Pulling out my coat, I pushed my arms inside.

"That's better. So where is the pass?"

"I don't have a stupid pass!"

Conner blinked at me and took my hand. "Got gloves?" he asked.

"At home. That's where I'm going."

"And after that?" It was incredible really, this cop treatment, but I wasn't even mad. It was just nice having Conner standing next to me, breathing in the same air, smelling of his aftershave.

"I don't know."

"How come you're cutting class?"

"I can't tell you." Conner walked with me, and as we passed the school and headed to my place,

I wondered if I should tell him, or if he already knew just like he'd known somehow that I'd been cutting class.

"It's that dead girl, huh?"

"How did you know?"

We turned the corner and I dared not look at him.

"I have been watching you," he said.

The comment didn't strike me as creepy or anything. I was just glad that he'd been watching me. I was gladder than I could say. As we walked, the feel of Conner's hand made me feel special somehow, as if he liked me so much he was willing to take the risk of leaving the school grounds with me. As we reached the house I stopped.

"My house is right there," I said, pointing to the white house with the high-pitched roof and white porch. In the spring and summer there would be time to sit outside and read a book or listen to music or just dream, but not now.

"I know," he said, drawing me close to him. We were on the sidewalk, only five doors down from my house. Mrs. Randall lived there, right where we'd stopped. She was a widow and lived alone but I hoped she wasn't standing near her front window.

I could feel the closeness of Conner's face, the smell of his aftershave, even before he kissed me.

The kiss was warm and long, and this time I closed my eyes and took it all in. His arms drew me closer, and he kissed me a second time and a third. When I opened my eyes, taking a short breath, he smiled into my eyes and kissed me again. I couldn't believe it. I couldn't believe I was here, and I couldn't believe I was with him.

He touched my hair, and it was all I could do to keep my feet planted on the ground. We were more than likely standing in the cold snow, but I didn't care. I laughed suddenly, and he pulled me from him, looking again into my eyes.

"So?"

"So, what?" I offered, though I wasn't sure where I'd managed to find my voice.

"You're laughing. So, kissing is funny to you?"

"No. I mean, yes. I mean, I don't know."

"You're thinking I should be turning green," he said.

"Green?"

"A frog?"

"No." I laughed again, this time, thinking of the experiment." I mean, I really wanted you to kiss me but I didn't think you ever would."

"Why not?"

"It's obvious."

"What's obvious?" He removed his arms from my waist although I didn't want him to and took my hand. "You are great and I thought it was about time I kissed you. Now, what about that date?"

***

That Friday was unlike any other I had previously experienced. I searched for my gloves, found them drying on the heat vent, and together we went in search of clues. I showed Conner the clues on my computer, including the photo in my purse, and managed to tell him everything I knew about the murder of Audrey Wilkins, including showing him the keychain I'd found near her body.

And Conner? Well, I would be lying if I didn't tell you he was impressed. As the time approached for school to end I suggested it was time for him to go home. He didn't fight me on it, but just smiled at me, kissed me one last time at the door, and left me watching him as he walked out of sight.

I had missed English class and lunch, and hadn't returned for art class. Mr. Cordial would surely have noticed, and my P. E. teacher Mrs. Langston would have taken note, as would the choir director and history teacher, but somehow, I didn't care.

Noteworthy

Passing notes was sort of juvenile and something I had never done before, but passing notes with Conner Ryan was another story.

We were in our own world now, filled with color and breathless moments, and time, well, there was no time. No school and practically nothing else.

I say that because I was still interested in finding out the mystery that had been on my shoulders for weeks now. But I was also interested in living in the moment with Conner and enjoying Christmas.

School would soon be out for winter break, but not before my mom and dad had received a note of their own concerning my missed classes. So, I'd been found out.

No matter. It seemed nothing mattered when I was with Conner.

Perhaps you get it, but even if you don't, you need to know that I was falling in love with him. We'd been on two dates, and though my dad hadn't yet met him, I was ready to show him off to a crowd. Our family Christmas party was coming up and it created a perfect opportunity to calm my mother's nerves, and allow my father to see how much better I could be than Oscar in choosing someone to date.

No, they wouldn't know – yet – how serious Conner and I had become the past few days, but they would at least know that I was dating and who I was with – something Oscar had never shared.

"I can't," he began.

"Can't meet my parents?" We were sitting on the swing out front on the porch, breaking it in so to speak. In moments, my mom and dad would be returning from work – maybe even Oscar would show up on time for once in his life and Conner could meet him.

"Oh, I can do that, just not the Christmas thing."

"Oh."

"I have other plans, with… with my own family."

"So maybe – "

"No. You need to go to your family party. I'll go to mine. We'll see each other on Christmas."

"Okay." I was disappointed, and I knew Conner could feel it. He seemed to know me in a deep way, and I often thought about how much he had begun to care for me in such a short time. My mom would never have believed it, though her experience with dad had been nothing short of miraculous; a cup of sugar. The romance had begun with a cup of sugar?

I knew the story by heart – and it was sort of funny that I knew it, but not in a *ha-ha* sort of way. It's just that finding Dad, for my mother, hadn't been easy, not easy like this. It had taken work, a divorce from her first husband, and plenty of time.

Could love be easy too?

When my parents drove up, Dad made his way to the porch first. With his hand outstretched, he asked, "So, who is this fine young man?"

I could have barfed. It was the most formal, awful thing my father could have said.

"Conner, sir."

Dad smiled, probably thinking of the phone call Conner had made previously to see if he could date me.

"Conner, what?" Mom asked, had to ask. She had met him. What was all the questioning about?

"Conner Ryan," Conner answered, shaking my Mom's hand.

"Well, well," Dad said, reaching for Conner's hand.

I had no idea what 'well, well' meant. But I cared what Dad thought about all of the things that mattered to me. And Conner mattered to me. Had I made a good choice? Was he happy that I hadn't hidden Conner away? Still, the words nagged at me through dinner. Conner had been invited to eat with us and Oscar; he'd finally shown up when we were ready to clean up.

Oscar removed his coat, dropped it on the floor by his chair, and sat down. "OH, hi. How have you been?" he asked, looking at Conner – much too knowingly, I thought.

"Oscar. . . So, this is your *sister*?"

"The very same."

Conner gave me the once-over and returned his gaze to Oscar. "How have you been?"

"Good. You?"

Oscar wiped at his hair. It had grown longer since we'd moved to Utah, and he had decided to let it grow out.

"Good."

"You know each other?" Mom asked.

Oscar sat down. "What's for dinner?" he asked.

Conner laughed. "Sorry, Mrs. James, he's always been like that."

Mom smiled. "Always – so, how do you two know each other?"

Oscar slid the casserole dish his way. There was one small piece left. He placed it on his plate and reached for the vegetables. A long time."

"How long?"

"About five years give or take."

"Five years?"

"We knew each other in Jersey," Oscar said. "I had no idea Conner had moved out here."

"This past summer."

"Wow." Oscar took a bite." I mean, from clear across the country almost."

"Well, so did you," Conner laughed.

"Right." Oscar took another bite.

"Did your parents end up getting divorced?" Oscar asked.

"Sort of; they're still separated."

"Sorry."

"Your parents are separated?" I asked, trying not to sound too upset. Conner had talked about having a family party, and not coming to mine because of it. How did that work when two parents were separated from each other?

"Sorry I didn't tell you."

"That's okay."

"I probably shouldn't have said anything." Oscar took another bite and a sip of water." I mean, it was tough, is probably still tough."

"Sometimes." Conner stood. "Can I help clean up?" he asked.

"Sure." I stood as well, hoping that the air would clear a bit. All this talk about divorce and separation had made my stomach queasy.

Conner was silent during clean up and I wondered what sort of terrible weapon Oscar had wielded. But it wasn't until later that night that I found out.

***

"You know what's funny?"

We were sitting outside again, our coats, scarves and hats doing their best at keeping us warm. But in a funny way I was still warm. Conner's arm was around me and there was no space between us as we sat together.

"I didn't even connect your last name. I mean, I spent a lot of time with your brother back in Jersey. We even went to parties together, liked some of the same girls."

"What girls?"

"I shouldn't have told you."

"What girls?"

"It doesn't matter, does it? What matters is that all of those times I was with your brother I never noticed you."

"Oh."

"What I mean is, I was never at your house to notice you. But didn't you come to that party?"

"What party?"

"The one that caused all of the problems?"

"You mean the one where I met Roxanne?"

"Yes!"

"That – was you?"

"I guess. What were *you* doing at the party?"

"Like I said, I came with my brother."

"You couldn't have. *I* came with your brother."

"Oh."

Conner was deathly pale. If I hadn't known better, I would have expected him to die right there in the swing. But then he blinked." I must have met your brother there... that time," he said, touching my hand. "That's the only thing that makes sense. And you were much younger then. That's probably why I never really noticed you."

"I guess."

Conner took a deep breath. "This is crazy. What are the chances?"

"That's just what I was thinking," I said, wondering to myself why Conner *hadn't* noticed me. I was his age after all, and he was far too young to be interested in the girls my brother was interested in. Something about his comments just didn't make sense to me.

"So, how did you meet my brother?" I asked.

Conner shrugged." I don't know. I mean, I must have seen him around, maybe at another party. I snuck around a lot then; had to. My mom and dad were constantly yelling at each other – I had to get out of the house."

My nerves, once revved up, smoothed down some. So, that was it. He had just been trying to escape his horrible home life. That was something I could understand.

"So, where are your parents now? I mean, who do you live with?"

Conner hesitated, and drew me closer to him if that's possible. "With my dad, mostly. Mom didn't come out with us, preferring the distance, but dad has allowed me to make one visit since summer."

"Oh. How is she doing?"

"Fine, I guess. When I was there she just wanted to know how I was doing. I told her, fine, what else was I supposed to say? But that was before I met you." Conner squeezed me tightly. "Are you getting cold?"

Actually, my feet were, they felt like bricks. "Want to go back in?"

He touched my hand, drawing me in again." I probably need to go. Dad gets mad when I'm out too late. He always thinks I'm at a party. What time should I come on Christmas?"

"Any old time."

"I don't want to get here before Santa shows up."

I punched him in the arm. He smiled over at me. "Just come about lunch time," I said, wondering to myself if Mom and Dad would care that he was coming. I hadn't asked them, but I felt as if the dinner had gone smoothly enough for them not to be bothered by it. Still, after Conner left I asked Mom if it was okay.

"What time?"

"I told him noon."

"That should be fine," she said. "He seems nice."

"He is nice," I answered, thinking of the kiss he'd given me just before leaving. I was drifting in and out of the thoughts of it when Oscar walked by. "You'd better be careful with that one," he said." I know more about him than I care to."

My heart stopped. I didn't know what to say. I almost didn't even want to know. If the things my

70

brother knew were terrible, maybe Conner had grown out of them. Maybe he was different – changed – he sure treated me with respect. I looked into my brother's eyes, but he wasn't smiling. He seemed dead serious about what he'd just told me.

"So, what should I be worried about?" I asked.

"That guy was into every drug on the planet; and every girl."

"Oh."

"I haven't seen him since before summer, since we moved, but the last time we partied he was drunker than a horse."

"You mean a skunk," I said, trying to lighten the sudden dark mood that surrounded me.

"No, a horse; skunks are too small of an animal for what he was doing."

"Oh."

Oscar shrugged." I don't know, he seemed nice enough tonight, but I would watch him."

Mom was still standing with us and I wondered what she was thinking. She was silent as death. Dad wasn't around, he wouldn't have been near as worried, and I suddenly wished that he'd been standing in the kitchen instead of Mom. But, so it was. Mom looked over at me briefly and then made her way to the kitchen sink where dirty dishes were waiting.

Oscar turned from me and walked to the fridge, grabbing a soda. I made my way down the hall into my room thinking about Jordan, the kid from art class who'd also warned me about Conner. What did he know that I didn't? It was just my luck to fall in love with someone who was trouble, or was he?

***

Christmas came and went like a winter storm, and though I felt as if things were going to be fine with Conner, something kept nagging me at the back of my neck, crawling into my hair and making my skin itch.

Conner was a true gentleman and we spent hours together, even after returning to school after the new year. We spent time working on the murder case and working on homework together. Jordan hadn't said another word about Conner and neither had my brother. Unfortunately, because Mom knew I'd been skipping class, she watched me like a hawk.

Conner and I had to use evenings and weekends to work through the clues, and, quite honestly, I didn't mind that so much. Still, Mom was pretty upset and Dad, well, he'd managed to sit me down in my room soon after Mom told him and pretty much had given me the lecture treatment.

It was sort of a kind lecture treatment, but still a lecture. I knew I deserved it, but the case was going by much slower since we had fewer daylight hours to do it.

It was about this time that I lost the sun keychain, though I looked in every place I could think of, including under my bed, I'd come away empty handed. I still had the pictures in my top dresser drawer, and Conner and I had discovered that the killer had more than likely worn Northway brand shoes at the time he'd killed Audrey Wilkins. Still, I was more than concerned that I didn't have the keychain. Sure, I had the one my mom had bought for me, but it wasn't the same. The engraving was important to this case, and if I didn't have the keychain, neither did I have the words, "I am not a morning person," on the back.

It was interesting, and more than a little revealing to me, that a morning person like Audrey would have a keychain with those words on it. I wondered again if the keychain had been a gift, or if she'd managed to buy it for herself for sentimental reasons. But what sentimental reasons, if it appeared she preferred running in the morning? When I'd asked Conner about it, he'd only shrugged.

"Beats me," he'd said.

And I could only shrug myself, wishing I could hop into his brain and see what he was really thinking.

Today, we'd located a store – not in the mall – but a store nonetheless that sold tie-dyed shoelaces. It was a shoe store of all things, and the woman behind the counter had nothing to tell us about who had purchased tie-dyed shoe laces lately, though she did admit that the laces had been around for a while – at least since summer – and that it was almost time to order new laces.

I thanked her and we left the building. We still didn't know anything about the tie-dyed sweat shirt or black sweat pants, but I was surer every day as I looked at the picture of Audrey Wilkins that I'd taken just before the police showed up, that the killer had set her up just like that, and that the sun keychain hidden in the snowball connected the two of them.

I'd shared the idea with Conner, and he'd agreed.

My parents had decided to help us with the case against my better judgment, mostly because I wanted to do this one on my own. I wanted to prove to my parents that I could do it, so I wasn't very excited about their interest at first. Still, after ditching class so many times they'd spoken to me about their assistance as if helping me was the only way they'd be able to keep close tabs on me, like I was a criminal or something.

I wondered what teacher had found out about my sneaking out, and what he/she was telling the other teachers, but as I returned to school that first week after the holidays, not one of them approached me about it.

I figured I was off the hook until Jordan came up to me with a smile.

"You know, you couldn't have managed it forever," he said.

"Managed what?"

We were standing in the hall right before art class. I tried not to stare at Jordan's yellow teeth or breathe in his awkward smell – a smell that reminded me of dead things left in the closet.

"Sneaking out; I warned you about Conner."

"So, it was you."

He exhaled a sickly odor and continued: "You would have been found out anyway. I just made it easier for you. You should be thanking me."

"Thanking you – for what?" I said.

The bell rang, and two students pushed past me and into class.

"That Conner is real trouble. Believe me."

"Why should I?"

Another student brushed past and I looked inside the room. Mr. Cordial was staring over at us.

"We'd better go in," I said, turning from Jordan and making my way to the door.

"You might not believe me now, but you will," Jordan said, as I made my way to my desk.

Fear

By mid-January my parents had discovered a key fact in the case, one which I tried to forget. The keychain hadn't been a gift to Audrey. Actually, the keychain had belonged to her boyfriend.

Audrey's parents had finally confessed.

The day me and my mom had gone shopping at the mall and discovered that Audrey's parents owned *Clarities* and that the keychain had been purchased there, Mrs. Wilkins had actually gone pale as she spoke to us about the keychain. Not admitting that a similar keychain belonged to her daughter, there yet had been an obvious connection, a connection that I had thought about for weeks.

Why hadn't I thought to confront the parents?

Probably for the same reason I rarely confronted my own: fear. But not the sort of fear that came when something dark and mysterious was following after me – no, more of a grownup-to-teen sort of thing. What did I know anyway, about solving a murder?

The online paper was still clueless as to the murderer of Audrey Wilkins, though there had finally been some speculation about her hair being pasted to the snow like the sun's rays and the knife wound on her back that was a different shape than knives found typically in a kitchen cupboard.

As my parents had explained it, they had gone to visit Carol and Carl Wilkins, and when her parents had finally revealed the truth, it had caused my Mom to hold Dad's hand even more tightly. The keychain had been purchased by Audrey herself and given to her boyfriend.

The news of it sent chills up my back. Had her boyfriend killed her? A sudden flash of Conner Ryan sent additional chills up my back. Conner wouldn't do anything like that, would he? Even in a drunken state? When on drugs?

"So, who was Audrey's boyfriend?" I asked her.

"Some boy by the name of Jordan Elspie."

"Jordan?"

"Yes. He's a little older than Audrey."

My heart stopped. It couldn't be. How could Jordan be Audrey Wilkins' boyfriend? The two of them together just didn't make sense. It had to be another Jordan.

"Evidently, because he's under-age, the police had to keep their mouths shut. The boy has been spoken to, of course, but his name won't be released to the general public."

"So, why did they tell *you*?"

I waited, trying to breathe easily, to make the question sound generic enough for my parents to feel as if this was just the next natural question to ask. But all I could think about was the guy in my art class, the one who'd tried to convince me to stay away from Conner.

And then my mom surprised me even more.

"I'm sorry, Brianne, I should have asked."

"About what?"

"About the keychain. I'm sorry. I found it in your backpack and I…"

"What?"

My mom reached into her purse and took it out." I just had a feeling about this."

I was livid now.

"What else have you taken?"

"Nothing. Promise."

I grabbed the keychain from her fingers and turned it over. The words, "*I am not a morning person*," leapt into my heart and hung on for dear life." I can't believe you did this."

"Well, we did find out something pretty important. That must count for something."

I pursed my lips, trying to remain calm. I was still being watched like a hawk, still didn't have all of the time I needed to work on this case, and now I find out that I couldn't even trust my own mother?

Mom reached for me, her cold hand on my cheek. "I'm so sorry."

Tears formed in my eyes.

"I...Mom, how could you do it? This was my case anyway. You and Dad can just bug off!" I could have said some other choice words but I restrained myself.

"Look, why don't we work on this together? As you recall, you were sneaking around for weeks, when your dad and I could have been helping you. We both need to be honest with each other."

I took a deep, cleansing breath, the sort of breathing I did just before I ran, and looked my mom square in the eyes." I need to trust you," I said.

"And, we need to trust you," she repeated, but not before my dad swept in, smiles and all.

"So, are we ready to sleuth together?"

"What?" My dad was so funny, so stupid sometimes.

"You know. Get this mystery solved once and for all?"

***

I don't know why I was afraid to go to school after the news of the keychain, but I was. Perhaps it was because I would have to sneak over, peek at Jordan's artwork or something. I'd just finished my portrait – late. His had been turned in more-than-likely weeks ago, and we were on sculptures now.

Still, maybe he had his painting in his art bin or something.

It was with trepidation that I entered the room early – the first bell had rung – and most students were still talking at their lockers in the hall. Mr. Cordial hadn't arrived yet and I was practically alone. The room smelled of clay and dampness, and as I walked to the back of the room all I could think about was Jordan's smell and yellow teeth. Audrey couldn't like a boy like Jordan, could she?

Reaching the back, I searched for Jordan's name on the bin. There it was two bins from the left. I looked inside. There were paints, a brush or two, clay in a ball like a grand marble, but no paper; nothing with his last name on it that I could see.

I checked the table near the back wall again, nothing.

I had almost given up hope when it occurred to me to check the drawings on the walls. We had done some shape work at the beginning of the year and some of the better drawings were there. I hadn't looked at any of them closely until now.

I'd looked through two pictures before the noise in the room grew. Moments later, bell two had rung, and I was still looking at the pictures when I saw it; his name.

Jordan *Elspie.*

Holy crap. Holy crap! *Really?* Audrey's boyfriend had been Jordan *Elspie*? I turned from the drawing and looked out at the class. Everyone was staring at me. I felt faint. Sick. I had to remind myself to breathe.

"You look sick," Mr. Cordial said.

I wandered to my seat, sat down, and tried not to stare at Jordan just two seats to the left. But I could feel his eyes on me, and they were like fire. What would cause a girl like Audrey to like a smelly boy like Jordan? It just didn't make sense.

***

"He's what?"

Conner breathed on me, his minty breath taking me in, hoping for a kiss. Only I didn't give it.

"Jordan Elspie was Audrey's boyfriend."

Conner's face blanched. "What?"

"I couldn't believe it either. But somehow, the two of them became, you know, a couple."

We were eating lunch together near the back of the room and I could distinctly see Jordan's head three rows up. He was sitting alone, eating something out of a crumpled bag.

"So, have you talked with him?"

I chewed my last bite of spaghetti and looked over at him. "Have any chocolate?" I asked him, thinking of his deep brown eyes and how hungry I suddenly was.

"No. Jeez, Brianne, what's going on?" He leaned in.

"I'm scared," I replied.

"Of Jordan?"

I nodded.

"Why?"

I turned my eyes in Jordan's direction and it struck me now, struck me harder than any clue I'd managed to learn so far. Jordan was small. Small!

"How tall do you figure he is?"

Conner took a sip of milk. "OH, I don't know, about 5'3" or so. Why?"

"Those prints found at the murder scene were quite large. They were deep, too. How big are Jordan's feet?"

"How am I supposed to know?"

"I bet they're small. And that he doesn't weigh much."

"Maybe a hundred pounds."

"Right. So, if Jordan's feet are small, I don't think he could have killed Audrey."

"Wait a second!" Conner held up his hands. "Are you saying, that before now you thought he might be the killer?"

"That keychain being his, what was I supposed to think?" I asked, taking a sip of my own milk. "What about the chocolate?"

"What? I don't have any. I told you that."

"Right." My heart was still beating as if it was going to jump out of my chest. Well, if Jordan wasn't the killer, why was his keychain found near Audrey's head by that huge tree? Why didn't *he* have it?

Conner touched my hand. "You should see your face," he said, leaning in and giving me a kiss. There was a "woo-woo" sound from somewhere in the room but I didn't turn my head to look. Conner lifted my plate, placed it and my milk carton and silverware on his tray, and shoved my tray underneath it.

He stood. "Follow me," he said, making his way to the area where trays were deposited. I stood up, watched him as he made his way to the drop-off point, and finally caught up with him after he was finished.

He took my hand. "I'll help you," he said.

"Help me with what?"

"See, he's still eating. We're going to walk over there and take a gander at his feet."

"A what?"

"A ga – a look."

"Why?" My legs were shaking.

"Look. He's probably not the killer. From what you've said, the killer had to have carried Audrey to the frozen stream, and that means strength. He's got to have big feet, and he has to weigh something substantial. You don't know why Audrey had the keychain. So, you need to ask him."

"But not – here."

"Why not?"

The lunchroom was as loud as a concert and I couldn't see trying to talk to Jordan with the noise beating inside my head, but I didn't relay the same to Conner. Instead, I followed his lead to Jordan's table.

Jordan was frowning even before he spoke.

"What do you want?" he hissed.

I looked down at Jordan's feet; he was straddling the bench like a horse and it was easy to see his worn sneakers. But they were small, too small to have created the footprints found at the park." I have something that belongs to you," I said, reaching in my purse for the keychain. Without another word, I handed it to him.

Jordan paled. He reached for the keychain, and turned it over in his hands.

"Where did you get – this?" he asked, staring down at it. For the first time, I noticed his dirty fingernails, and the dull shine of grease within his hair.

"Near your girlfriend's dead body."

Jordan gasped, but he didn't look up.

"Perhaps you can tell us why we found this keychain near Audrey's body when it's yours," Conner said, causing Jordan to look up. There were tears in his eyes.

"She wasn't my girlfriend, well, not exactly. She was just helping me, that's all."

"Helping you with what?" I asked.

"None of your business. Didn't I tell you not to hang out with this creep?"

Conner slugged the boy on the arm. "Tell us or you're dead," he said.

It was a rude comment, one I would have never made myself, but perhaps it would get the boy talking. I looked into Jordan's eyes. For the first time, I noticed they were hazel, sort of a blue-brown, the color of a bush drying out in winter.

"Running. I was running with her."

I looked down at the boy's small form and wondered why he even needed to run.

"When was the last time you ran with her?"

"The day before she was found," he sniffed. "But you have to believe me; I would never hurt Audrey Wilkins. I loved her."

Conner laughed. It was an unkind laugh, sort of like a laugh you force that isn't real at all. I nudged him.

"What?" he asked.

Jordan stood." I need to get to class," he said, looking Conner directly in the eyes.

"Not until after you tell us why Audrey would have your keychain and not you," Conner said.

"We sort of got into a fight," Jordan said, turning from us. "But I didn't kill her."

Jordan grabbed his worn sack, but not before Conner had him by the shoulder. "Have you said anything to the police about the keychain?" he asked.

"No."

"Good." Conner released him.

"She was kind; always nice. The keychain was a gift. I wondered where it had gone."

Jordan looked into my eyes. "Thank you for returning it to me," he sniffed, glaring over at Conner for one brief moment.

Part of me wanted to ask for the keychain back. It was evidence after all, and I hadn't even planned on giving it to him. Why had I? In the end, Jordan left us both with the sun keychain pushed inside his worn jean pocket, and all I could think about was losing a valuable piece of evidence.

Still, I knew what it looked like, what the inscription revealed about the owner, and I had an almost-duplicate copy of the same thing. What was there to worry about?

Questions Worth Asking

For days after the confrontation with Jordan Elspie, I thought about Conner Ryan and how he'd treated him. I even considered talking to him about it. But, I reasoned, he had always been kind to me. Maybe he'd merely been trying to protect me from Jordan Elspie or something.

Still, as the days wore on, I couldn't help but revisit that day every time I walked into the lunchroom and found Jordan sitting alone, another worn lunch sack in front of him.

I wanted to ask Conner why he'd really gotten so forceful with Jordan that day and why he'd asked that question about whether or not the police knew about the keychain, but I didn't. I kept the thought welled up inside of me, and there were days I wanted to release it, but I could never bring myself to do it.

It was nice being around Conner. When we were alone, magic happened, and he was a pretty good detective, too. I just didn't know how I could live my life like I used to if he ever left me. And so, we never spoke about Jordan Elspie. I talked to my parents about him, however – about the keychain and how I'd returned it. And my parents spoke about it to the police, but after that I didn't speak to Jordan, (though the police made it a point to speak to me about where I'd found it) and he made no effort to speak to me. It was as if I no longer existed in his eyes, and I was too busy with Conner and the case to really reflect on it much.

It was nearing the end of January, when Conner invited me to the school Valentine's dance and I accepted. This would be my first dance, and it was about time. I'd gone through years of school without getting asked to a dance, and I was excited. Better late than never, I thought.

Two weeks later, when Conner showed up at my front door, black tux and all, I tried not to swoon. Mom was standing behind me and I could feel her swooning for the both of us anyway. Dad was already in bed, though it was only 7 p. m. He'd returned home from work, sick, he said, but wished me well on my date.

I'd wanted to show him my new dress, a red, sparkly affair, and promised myself that I would show him later, or at least give him a copy of the picture of us together, and hoped he'd be awake later when I returned so that I could share my experience with him.

Mom was all aglow as she wished me well and shut the door behind us.

It had snowed the night before, and the yard and streets glittered from the streetlights. I looked up at

Conner. "You look beautiful," he said, taking me in a warm embrace. He kissed me, longer than usual, and I breathed in his minty aftershave.

Inside the car, I thought about how much I was growing to love him. He was everything I'd ever dreamed of, and I wondered, quite suddenly, what he really saw in me. I was, after all, pretty, but not beautiful. I wasn't popular like he was, and I was so different from any other girl he must have dated – I couldn't think of one that would enjoy dissecting frogs.

Still, maybe that's why Conner liked me. I was different.

As the car, (his own), crushed through the snow-packed streets, I was in a dream until the brakes were suddenly hit and I jerked forward. A car had suddenly stopped in front of us, and a man, larger than life it that's possible, stepped out.

He was wearing a thick, though threadbare coat, and his hands were bare.

"Hey!" Conner shrieked. "What are you doing!?"

The snow was so packed, it would have been difficult to get around the man's car on the narrow street, and so I waited, or tried to wait patiently as Conner yelled at the man, stepping out of the car and leaving me alone inside it with the driver's door still open.

"My cars stuck!" the man yelled. "Want to help me push it around the corner?"

"No! Just get it out of here!"

I watched as the man, alone, tried to get his old car out of the way. It was just too hard with the slick streets and the piled snow.

I got out of the car.

"What are you doing? Get back inside!" Conner yelled at me.

I ignored him. Lifting my red dress from the dirty snow, I tiptoed in my high heeled shoes to the back of the man's car. "Okay, go!" I yelled.

The wheels turned. Slush the size of baseballs heaved themselves against my legs and dress, but I continued to push. Nothing. And then, suddenly, the wheels released themselves and the car moved forward. I looked to my right. Conner had been pushing with me.

He glared over at me as the man thanked us and turned the corner. "I can't believe you did that!" he said, stomping back to the car and getting in, leaving me to watch him in my soiled dress. I just couldn't believe it. I couldn't believe – him.

I turned to the car, stepped slowly to it, and got inside, brushing some of the wetness off.

"Not in here," Conner said. "At the dance; use the bathroom."

He turned from me, his eyes still glaring.

I sat silently as he drove, not really believing what had happened. Did Conner have some real problem with the male population, or what? I'd never met his father, but perhaps he wasn't the best influence. Maybe Conner really wanted to live with his mother and for some reason, couldn't. All of these thoughts and more flew inside my brain until Conner parked the car at the school.

He got out and came around to my side. Opening the door, he barked: "Get out."

"No," I said.

"What?" He leaned in.

"No," I said. "Not until you apologize."

Conner laughed. "Come on, Brianne."

I stared into his luscious brown eyes, hardly believing we were having this conversation, but it had to be said. "Why did you want to know if the police had heard about Jordan's keychain?"

"What?"

"Well?"

"I…I don't know. It was just a question. Don't you want to clean off your dress?"

The chilly air was quickly filling the car. "Yes, but not until you give me an answer."

"I don't believe you. Aren't you cold?"

"Why were you concerned about the police knowing about Jordan's keychain?"

"I don't know."

"They know now anyway, but…"

"The police know?" Conner slammed the passenger side door and walked around the car. He opened his door and got in.

"Did you tell them?"

"No, my parents did."

"What, your parents know, too?"

"Of course, we're working together on this case."

Conner wiped at his eyes. In that moment, they didn't remind me of chocolate. I was so mad at him I could spit.

"I wish you hadn't done that." He looked ahead as if something or someone was approaching and then turned back to me. His eyes had softened.

"Really, Brianne, I thought I was helping you with this case."

"Because I invited you," I said.

Conner reached for the keys and turned the ignition. The car spurted to a start. He reached for the heater, turning the knob. "Well, if you have to know," he said.

I waited. As the car warmed, Conner reached for my hand but I wouldn't give it. Something was strange, so strange here, and I was bound and determined not to go into the dance until we'd resolved whatever Conner Ryan was hiding from me. I would wait until hell froze over before I'd allow him to take me to the dance.

"I've known Jordan Elspie for long enough to believe he can't be trusted. If it wasn't for the fact that those footprints found at the crime scene were so large and that guy so weak, I would have pegged Jordan as the killer in a second. He lies through his teeth."

"How do you know? I mean…"

"Look, Brianne. I know you're a great detective and all, but maybe you should leave this one alone. Spend your time with me."

"Why?"

"Because I'm a nice guy, have terrific hair and have eyes that remind you of chocolate."

"Who told you that?"

"What?"

"About your eyes; I didn't tell you that."

"You must have."

"No." There was one thing I knew for sure, and that one thing was that I'd never voiced my opinion on Conner's eyes, I'd only thought it. Unless…"

"Have you been talking to my brother?" I asked.

"Sure. We went to a par – I mean, yes."

I was furious; there was no other emotion that could fill me. "What else has my brother told you?"

"Come on, Brianne."

"What I know about my brother is that he doesn't trust you. He warned me about you and now I see why."

"Oscar? He wouldn't do that. We're friends."

"Are you sure?"

"Are we going to fight all night, or go to the dance?"

I swallowed. The last thing I wanted was to fight all night with Conner, the guy I was falling in love with. Or, was I?

"Why were you so rude to Jordan Elspie?"

"He's a nerd. I don't like him."

"And the man, the one that was stuck in the snow and you wouldn't help, what's up with him? Do you know him or something?"

Conner was silent. "Of course not. He was just being a jerk."

"And you weren't?"

"Okay, so I got mad. I just didn't want to be late for the dance."

"Like that matters," I said, looking ahead of me and beyond the other side of the windshield. "The dance must be almost over anyway."

Conner looked over at the clock on the dashboard. "We're only a half hour late. Want to go in?"

I didn't but I nodded.

***

In the end, the dance helped to soothe my fears about Conner Ryan, though I wasn't completely sure if I could continue with him. I was mad at Oscar, had confronted him about his broken promise, and had spent some time with Dad, telling him about the good parts of the dance before I began to feel even an ounce of relief.

The dance had been beautiful after all, and the band terrific.

Still, I couldn't believe I still wanted to date Conner after all we'd been through. I'd heard about couples fighting – even my parents had had their limited share – but I didn't think it would ever really happen to me.

And then it came, the news that my Dad's new heart was failing.

I couldn't believe it, though I could. He had not looked well for months following the operation. He had been too tired, too pale, too everything, and not really a part of my life. I hated the situation. I hated him for getting sick.

Conner said he understood.

"It's your dad," he said, taking me in his arms on the porch swing as the white snow swirled beyond. "You love him."

"Would you feel bad if your dad died?" I asked.

Conner hesitated for only a moment." I suppose I would, even though he treats me like crap," he said, removing his arm from around my shoulders and folding his hands together. I could see the pain in his eyes, the way his eyes glazed over at the very thought of his father, and I think I knew even then about the pain he'd had. He would rather have lived with his mother.

But I didn't say anything. It was too hard, and the angry outbursts I had seen before I didn't want to see again – ever. I just wanted to live in this dream world with Conner, sitting on the swing, taking each other in, kissing. I wanted to hold his hand and have him tell me how beautiful I was. I wanted to believe it, all of it.

Officer Hybrid had invited me into the precinct an additional time, but I hadn't said anything to Conner.

And though the questions that I had been asked rang through my ears like a bugle, I didn't share what we'd spoken about with Conner.

I don't know if I decided consciously not to speak with Conner about the case unless he asked me about it, but it seemed to occur naturally, like winter turning to spring. I just knew that from then on, I would be working on the case without him.

The day following, I took some time to work on the clues I'd already gathered about the case. The man was large. He had big feet. Wore Northway shoes – Air Mine 95s – with a diamond sole; I'd discovered much of this information just this week, though he may have purchased them at a discount store. He didn't have much money, at least not enough to buy new tires for his car.

Audrey could have been murdered before they ever reached the park, the killer spreading out her hair on the cold earth before leaving her, but that didn't explain the keychain that I was pretty sure Audrey had left there. The tie-dyed shoe laces had more than likely been purchased at the local shoe store. What else? Oh yes, Audrey's red shoes. Kobear. I'd done a lot of searching on that, and my parents had checked with Audrey's parents as well – yes, the shoes were Kobear. She'd been found 30 minutes after her death, wore a tie dyed sweat shirt and matching laces, a red scarf around her neck made of wool. Her brown eyes had been open when I found her, and she'd been stabbed with a knife.

The fifteen-year-old lived in West Commons with her parents, Carol and Carl. They had money and luxuries I could only dream about. The girl loved jogging, as I did. She had taken Jordan Elspie under her wing and they'd spent some time jogging together. She'd given him a sun keychain that strangely had been found at the creek inside a snowball, and Jordan had sworn to her that he wasn't the killer. Even the cops, it seemed, had ruled him out, but maybe their eyes were suddenly open again since the discovery of the keychain.

Many questions still remained. Why the keychain at Montgomery Park? Jordan said he'd lost it and that he didn't know where it was. But even if he did know, and wasn't telling me the truth, he still couldn't have killed Audrey Wilkins. He simply wasn't strong enough to lift her. His feet – about a men's size 7 – couldn't have made those footprints I'd seen that morning by the frozen stream.

So, if it wasn't him, then who?

Someone with a motive. Someone who needed her dead.

The police had wanted to know more about the keychain, how I'd found it and what I thought of the meaning behind, "I'm not a morning person." They wanted to know why it was inside a snowball, and why it appeared that Audrey's hair was fanned out just like the sun keychain. Did I see a connection?

It was strange and wonderful at the same time.

Perhaps I wasn't such a bad detective after all, because all of these things I had already asked myself. But I had no real answers for the police, and finally, Officer Hybrid, with his large eyes and gray eyebrows that made me think of a witch's broom, told me that I could leave.

I walked out of the police station, wondering again how this entire thing would finally be solved, and thought of Oscar. I really hadn't spoken to him in weeks. Sure, I'd gotten angry with him for telling Conner Ryan my secret. But I hadn't really talked to him about why he worried about me and Conner so much.

Now was the time.

I walked inside the house, down the hall and to Oscar's door. It was shut. I knocked, hoping he was there, hoping that he had at least a couple of minutes for me.

In seconds, the door clicked open. Oscar leaned out.

"What do you want?" he asked. He looked tired and I wondered if I'd woken him up.

"I came… to apologize," I said, though the words had just come to me in that moment. I'd wondered all the way home how I was going to approach my brother, and then, as easy as making a sandwich, it had come to me.

"For what?"

"For getting mad at you about Conner."

"And?"

"And what? I confided in you. I didn't think you would tell him."

Oscar opened the door widely and invited me in. The room was a mess of clothes, towels and junk everywhere. He cleaned off a chair. "Sit," he said, walking me to the bed and sitting down." I only meant to bring you two, closer together. I thought you'd thank me."

"But I thought you had problems with him."

"I do, but you're my sister, you know. And besides, he may have changed."

"I wouldn't be so sure of that," I said, staring at the blinds that were raised crookedly at the window.

"What do you mean?" He sat straight. "He didn't hurt you, did he?"

"No, not exactly."

"Then, what?"

"I just need to know what you know about him."

"I've already told you. Drinking. Drugs. Women. What else is there?"

"I don't know me…"

"Has he hit you?"

"No, he just, well, he gets angry sometimes."

Oscar stood, his arms crossed over his chest. "He always did that. He's probably still angry about the divorce, and living with his dad."

"About that. What's his dad like?"

"Why do you want to know?"

"Just curious. If his dad is angry too, Conner's anger would make sense. Maybe we can help him."

"We?"

"Sure."

Oscar sat. "If Conner is yelling around you, I think you should leave him and the sooner the better."

"Why?"

I didn't really want to hear Oscar's answer, but in the deepest part of my soul I did. I was tired of not knowing. I needed some answers.

"His dad used to beat him. I don't know if he still does, but it used to happen all of the time."

"Conner would never hit me. He loves me."

Oscar blinked, but he didn't smile. "So, it's come to that, has it?"

I wasn't sure what Oscar meant exactly, but we'd come too far in the conversation for me to stop now. "Yes. And I think I love him, too."

"Be careful, sis."

"I will. Conner just seems to have some real trouble with men. He even appears to hate strangers," I said. "The other day he got real mad when a man blocked him in traffic. I thought he was going to kill him."

"Really?"

"We were going to the dance…"

"How was it?"

"Good. After we got there Conner was fine."

"Maybe I should talk to him."

"Who, Conner?"

"Yeah. Make sure he holds off when he's around you. Unless, that is, you're ready to leave him."

I wasn't, but I didn't say that to Oscar. He worried too much, and the rest of the time he was who knows where. Everything between Conner and me would work out – it just had to.

***

I was in art class when Jordan Elspie pulled me aside.

"So?"

I looked over at his clay encrusted hands. Projects were due next Tuesday and it was Friday. I'd barely started on my bowl and Jordan was almost ready for firing. He placed his hands under the faucet and began to wash the clay off.

I turned to go back to my project but Jordan's words made me stop. "Has he hit you yet?" he asked.

I stopped, turned and stared at him.

"You know that's next, don't you?"

"I don't know what you're talking about."

Jordan wiped his wet hands on a paper towel and scrunched the towel in his hands as he approached me. "He's got you pegged," came the reply." I would leave him if I were you."

"Well, I'm not you."

He shrugged. "Suit yourself."

I walked back to my desk, but Jordan's words swirled in my head and reminded me of the words of my brother. So, I was with a nice guy who'd never hurt me personally, but was known for his anger toward others. Well, maybe he was over all that. Maybe, just maybe being with me was better for him than his life and anger without me.

I'd just finished shaping my bowl when the bell rang. Mr. Cordial was standing at the front of the class and everyone, it seemed except me, was filing out – even Jordan, who I didn't know whether to like or hate.

Mr. Cordial blinked at me from the front of the room. "Better be cleaning up," he said. "You don't want to be late to your next class."

I was on high alert for most of the teachers – I don't know what they expected – that I'd ditch class again or something, but after an additional meeting with the principal, I assured him that I wouldn't be cutting class again, and I hadn't. Still, what had once been a warm smile and a friendly tone from Mr. Cordial had suddenly changed to occasional stares and worried looks.

Like now.

"Don't worry," I said, looking around me and discovering that we were the only two people left in the room. I thought again of my brother and Jordan Elspie, who appeared to have my best interests at heart. So, why did I feel so crappy?

***

"You're in a bad mood."

I turned to Conner. School was out and it was all I could do to smile back at him so that he wouldn't know how I was really feeling.

"Ready to do some sleuthing?"

I wasn't sure how I was going to get around this one. For a week, I hadn't said anything, and Conner and I had done different things. When I wasn't with him, I'd spent some time searching different places where Audrey might have purchased the tie-dyed sweat shirt with no results. My parents had asked to borrow the photos of Audrey Wilkins, and I'd discovered later that they'd taken them to the police. I was mad, but somehow, with all the other emotions inside me, I just couldn't bring myself to care too much.

I'd returned to *Clarities* and had had a few short moments with Carol Wilkins, had spent some time jogging at the park, stopping for a moment to look at the spot where I'd found Audrey, and had even thought about the keychain that was no longer in my possession.

Jordan Elspie was a freak and I just couldn't help feeling that way about him. For some strange reason, Audrey had felt sorry for him, and they'd become some sort of strange pair. I would have to talk to Jordan, but when and how? I could hardly stand him now.

I swallowed as Conner's hand found mine.

"You're a million miles away."

"Two."

"So, what's up?"

"I just don't feel like sleuthing today."

"Why not?"

We were almost to my house. He stopped me at the sidewalk where we'd first kissed. The memory of that moment warmed me, but Conner didn't kiss me now.

"You know, you haven't been the same this week."

"I know. I'm sorry."

"Maybe we should do some sleuthing."

I looked up at Conner, took in his face. His dark brown hair was a bit more wavy than usual. He was going to grow it out. His chocolate brown eyes were staring into my own.

"Maybe it's good you no longer have an interest in that girl. Let the police do what they're paid to do."

"I guess."

"Want to go ice skating?" He was staring down at me, grinning like the Cheshire cat.

"I guess." What I really wanted to do was be alone, but I couldn't say that to Conner, could I? I'd been silent with my feelings since talking to Oscar, and Jordan Elspie hadn't helped any. If there was any future sleuthing to do, I needed to talk with Jordan, and without Conner tagging along.

"You know, I'm pretty tired," I said. "Do you mind if we call it a night?"

"Really?"

"Really. You don't care, do you? I'd like to go to bed early."

"Okay." We stopped at my front door. "Are you okay?" he asked again, planting a quick kiss on my lips.

"Yes. Don't worry. I'll see you tomorrow?"

"Probably not." He looked away.

"Why?"

My dad says he needs me for some stuff."

"What kind of stuff?"

"I don't know, just stuff."

"Oh, okay."

Conner touched me lightly on the arm. "See you Monday?" he said.

***

Life is just weird, you know. One moment you are in love, the next you're wondering if what you felt was really love at all. As I shut the door that day, watching Conner walk out of sight, I wondered if I'd ever felt anything for him.

I wasn't mad at him, you have to know that. But I was suddenly not very happy with him either. I just couldn't get the words of my brother or the words of Jordan Elspie, out of my mind. If I was wrong and they were right, I might just be Conner Ryan's next victim, and one thing I'd learned from living with my first parents, is that people could get angry, very angry, and I didn't want to go through that ever again.

Pain

When I returned from sleuthing on Saturday afternoon, my dad was in the hospital. I'd received a text, evidently, but I hadn't heard the ping, and I'd been so intent on my newfound discoveries that I hadn't realized my mom had been trying to contact me until I returned home to find everyone gone.

Checking my phone, I saw the message.

"Dad's in the hospital. Come when you can." The message had been sent around noon.

Returning to the driveway, I jumped in Dad's car and started the engine. The drive was short to *Columbia Hospital*, but it felt longer that day, almost as if time had slowed down so that I could think about my life and what it would be like without a dad in it.

I'd never really had a dad until Henry came along. He was sweet and cared about me, I knew that. I knew he loved my mom and I knew he loved Oscar. I also knew that the words didn't come out much, but rather were showed by the respect he gave each of us for our privacy. While Mom hovered, he stood back and watched us, only stepping closer if he felt like we needed him.

Well, I needed him now, and he was in some hospital bed, probably hooked up to tubes like before. Probably not even awake; or dead.

Stopping at the light I looked down at my phone and checked for messages from my mom. Nothing.

The light changed and I drove the few extra blocks to *Columbia Hospital*. Stepping in the foyer, I enquired about Henry James and was told he was on the second floor, room 208. I took the elevator; it was miserably slow, but finally the silver doors opened and I walked out.

I saw Oscar first, his head between his arms, huddled in the chair like a ball. He didn't see me until after I'd tapped him on the shoulder. His eyes were red and filled with tears.

"Where have you been?" he asked, standing up and hugging me tightly. Oscar never hugged me – ever – and I was immediately worried.

"Where is Mom?"

"With Dad." He wiped at his eyes.

"What happened?"

"A heart-attack."

"Is Dad…?"

"He's okay, but Mom, she was pretty scared. I had to drive the car here. Mom was sobbing like there was no tomorrow."

Maybe there wasn't. If Dad died.

Oscar let go of me and sat down. I sat in the chair next to him. Only then did I notice all of the people in the room.

"So, what is happening with Dad?" I whispered.

"Last I heard he was breathing with a machine."

Oscar blinked, and huge tears fell from his eyes.

"So, he's not breathing on his own?"

"No, and he's all hooked up."

"I want to see him."

"They won't let you. Only Mom."

"I have to see him. Did you see him?"

"Yes, but they shoved me out."

"How long…"

Oscar looked up at the large clock. "About a half an hour now. Where were you?"

"Sorry. I was doing some stuff and didn't know a text had come in."

"Well, what about the call?"

"What call?"

"I called you right after I got here."

"No, you didn't."

I looked down at my phone and checked all of the numbers. Nothing had come from Oscar. "See?" I said, shoving the phone at him.

He looked at my phone briefly then checked his own. "OH, sorry. I guess I called someone else by mistake."

"Who?"

"Looks like Jeremy. I'd better call him."

Oscar talked to his friend, apologizing for the mix-up. He paled at something his friend said back. Once off of the phone, Oscar turned to me. "He's drunk," he said.

***

Ms. Meacham was beaming and I wondered if she'd recently gone on a date with Mr. Cordial. English was okay most of the time, but today I just couldn't focus.

Dad was still in the hospital, and Mom hadn't left his side since Saturday, but I was expected to return to school.

"The essay is due a week from this Friday," Miss Meacham was saying. Moaning erupted from the class, the standard fare for any assignment." I want you to write about your favorite hobby. It can be anything you like." She clasped her hands and looked towards the window. "Things are going to be warming up in the next few months, and I want to have something spectacular to show your parents come parent-teacher conferences."

Spectacular. Ha. I just didn't get it; it was like life was some sort of ray of sunshine or something. Jordan Elspie hadn't been too excited to see me, either, but I'd been jogging after all, and had more or less just stumbled upon him.

"So, what are you doing here?" I'd asked him. He was standing, of all places, at the spot where I'd found Audrey Wilkins. Just standing there like a frozen statue.

"Just thinking." Jordan looked over at the frozen stream that wasn't as frozen as in previous months. Some of the ice had actually broken and I could see water in-between the broken pieces. His hazel eyes took me in before returning his gaze on the partially frozen stream.

"What do you want?"

"I was just out running. Love it."

"Oh. So did Audrey. We were going to be married, you know."

"Married?"

"I bet you think that's pretty funny." He turned from the stream, tears falling down his cheeks." I bet you think all of this is funny."

"No."

"I bet you're wondering why a girl like Audrey could like a guy like me."

"No, I mean, yes."

Jordan wiped his face. "Figures. We were friends, but I knew that if we hung out long enough she would grow to love me like I loved her."

I wasn't sure what to say then. Jordan Elspie was a strange creature, one that I might never know or understand. But this was my perfect moment to do so. It was like God had suddenly granted me the desire of my heart to speak with him, and I needed to do things perfect so that Jordan would open up.

"How long did you know her?" I asked.

"Audrey? A long time. We were in grade school together. After that, we hung out sometimes, but things got strange when she got older."

"What do you mean?"

Jordan sniffed and wiped his nose on his coat sleeve. For the first time, I noticed how worn it was. It was also too small; his wrists peeking out especially when his arms were down.

"She was too popular for me by then, but I couldn't believe she would really leave me. We were friends, after all. I guess I bugged her too much or something, because one day she said our friendship was over, just like that. She said not to bother her anymore."

"I bet that hurt."

Jordan reached into his pocket and pulled out the keychain. "And then this summer, she came over to my place. I almost couldn't breathe. She handed me this. I looked down at it and almost laughed at the words that she'd engraved. 'I am not a morning person.' I laughed so hard I started crying. She came up to me then, took me in her arms and told me that she was sorry; that we could still be friends. I loved her for that."

"You're not a morning person then?"

"Oh, no. Far from it. I feel bad about that, too, because she always liked to run in the morning, but I didn't like mornings and when she decided to run with me we would meet here – she sometimes gave up her mornings to run with me, isn't that great? We would

111

come here, just the two of us. Summers were the worst. Even though neither of us had school I liked sleeping in. Sometimes it got so hot. But Audrey never complained. Never…"

I looked again in the partially frozen stream and thought about where I'd found the keychain. I wondered once again who had placed it inside the snowball and why.

"One morning I fished inside my backpack for the keychain but I couldn't find it. It was gone. I asked Audrey about it but she didn't know. A week later, she was found dead here."

"Did you have anything else on the keychain, a key perhaps?"

Jordan's eyes shot in my direction. "Of course, she'd also given me a key to her house."

My heart thumped.

"So where is the key now?"

"I was going to ask you that when you returned the keychain to me, but something didn't feel right. Conner Ryan didn't feel right."

"What do you have against him anyway?" I asked.

"Lots of things. Mainly, that he hits girls."

"Oh."

"And he doesn't like me. I don't know why, but lots of people don't like me. You don't."

"I…" The words had caught in my throat then, and in the moment, I thought about the reply I needed to

112

give to Jordan Elspie, I heard another voice. It was Miss Meacham and she was speaking to me.

"Brianne? Do you want to be a part of this conversation?"

I'd been scribbling in my notebook, dreaming of my Saturday visit with Jordan. I hadn't heard a thing that she'd said and wondered how long I'd been lost in my thoughts. The class was laughing.

"Yes?" I asked.

***

The other part of my conversation with Jordan Elspie, the part that I didn't get to, went a little like this:

"I'm sorry," I said when Jordan asked me if I liked him because I really didn't like him – much. He was the strangest, skinniest, dirtiest guy I'd ever laid eyes on.

"I knew it. So why are you talking to me now?"

"I don't know I…"

"Sure, you do." He scuffed his worn shoe against the snow that was fading just a bit. I could finally see yellow grass strands where he'd lifted the snow. "You want to know if I killed her."

"No, really, I…"

"I know you don't like me, but you can at least tell me the truth."

"Sorry," I said again, looking out towards the semi-frozen stream again. "So why do you think the

113

killer brought Audrey here? And why do you think he hid the keychain in the snowball?"

"Is that what he did?"

In that moment, I realized Jordan had known nothing about the snowball, only that I'd managed to get the keychain for him somehow. For all intents and purposes, I could have been the killer. I was struck dumb with the thought.

"It was right there by this tree." I pointed to the spot. The snow was practically gone. Only some crusty ice remained.

"Why would he do that?" Jordan asked.

"So, you think it's a he?" I said.

"Sure, don't you?"

"I don't know what I think. Actually, it's probably a man because the footprints leading to and from Audrey's body were quite large. A small person could never have carried her to this spot."

"You mean, like me."

I tried to smile, but the smile felt forced. Instead, I stared at the spot where Audrey had been put, trying to remember every detail about how she'd been laying. "So, what did you think about her hair?" I asked.

"It was beautiful. I loved it."

"No, I mean, the way it was fanned out around her."

"It was fanned out?"

"Yeah. Just like the sun keychain."

"Wow, that's weird, even for me," Jordan said.

Jordan told me about the key to Audrey's house – how he wondered why the keychain was keyless when I'd returned it to him, but again, Conner had prevented him from speaking up about it, he said.

"Just so, you know, I don't think you did it," I said.

Jordan blinked at me, his hazel eyes glaring. "That's only because I'm too small to have carried her," he said, "not because you think I could never do a terrible thing like that."

I hesitated. What could I say? I couldn't lie to Jordan, he would know. And so, I told him the truth. It was probably the first truth he'd ever heard from me. "You're right, but I want to change that. Maybe we can be friends."

Jordan smiled. "You don't mind that I'm small and poor and stuff?"

I looked over at Jordan's coat, and then down at his shoes. Christmas had come and gone and I'd been so wrapped in my love for Conner that my thoughts had gone little beyond him. But now – now, I wished that I'd done something for Jordan Elspie.

I reached out my hand. "Friends," I said.

Jealousy

"I can't believe you're talking to that guy."

"You mean, Jordan?" I said. We were on the swing outside my place as always and I'd spent little time with Conner the last couple of weeks. We'd talked by phone and we'd had only one date to see a movie, but beyond that I'd been busy with the case.

And so had my parents. Evidently, Jordan Elspie had once been the number one suspect; that is, until the police had put two and two together and had come up with five. For one, the killer had to have been someone who could drive – unless they'd driven Audrey to Montgomery Park without a driver's license. Two, the killer had large feet. And three, the stabbing was deep enough in Audrey's back to warrant someone older or at least with some brute strength that could do it.

"Do you like him?" Conner asked. He was as far away from me as possible on the little swing, but still close enough to get in my face.

"Of course, I do. Jordan's nice."

"I thought you didn't like him."

"So did I."

"And now?" Conner breathed out and stared into my eyes. I could hardly believe it. He was jealous.

"He's just a friend. Really, Conner."

"Good. I wouldn't want to have to smack him upside the head."

"Conner!"

Conner smiled at me wearily. "Really, Brianne, you are so stupid sometimes. I was just kidding. I knew you could never like a guy – like that."

"Like what?"

"Greasy hair, smelly, you know; homeless."

"Jordan is homeless?"

Conner smirked." I thought you knew."

"I didn't. I…"

"Look, that kid has been trouble to me since day one. People take him in all the time, trying to help, but the kid is hopeless. His father is hopeless."

"You know his father."

"Sure. So?"

"Where do they live?"

"I told you Jordan's homeless."

"Who takes them in?"

"How should I know? We're not."

"So, how do you know people are taking them in?"

"Just Jordan."

"So, how do you know that?"

"Talk. You should listen sometime."

I couldn't believe what I was hearing. Where was the cool Conner that I'd met just a few months ago? Where were his kind words for me now? He'd never called me stupid. He'd never told me that I wasn't a good listener.

He reached for me, scooting closer. "Sorry," he said, squeezing my hand a little too hard, "I guess I was just a little jealous. You've been spending more time with Jordan than with me lately."

"I have not."

"Now you're lying. Is he helping you with the case?"

"No," I lied. I was getting better at lying, but tried to avert my eyes from Conner's.

Conner released my hand. "You know, I would like to help again," he said, turning to face me and looking into my eyes. As in many times previous, I looked into his eyes that reminded me of chocolate. Only, this time, surprisingly, I was thinking of mud.

"Why are you smiling?" he asked.

"No reason."

"Then stand up so I can kiss you."

There was a power in Conner that I couldn't resist even though I worried about the direction our love was taking. Love wasn't easy, no matter the form. Conner took me in his arms and kissed me heavily on the lips. When I was finally able to come up for air he was smiling down at me. "Now, that's better," he said, stroking my hair.

The kiss was good as always, but when he was gone I went into my room and snuggled under my blankets thinking of Jordan Elspie and how I could help him.

***

"Want to meet after school?" Jordan asked. We were standing in the hall; Conner hadn't yet come for me.

"Sure; at the tree?"

Jordan nodded. It was our favorite place.

Today, in P. E., we were actually doing some weight lifting. We'd been invited or something equally lame by the teacher of that class, and I wasn't looking forward to it. People would be staring as I lifted, and since I was the *weakest link* I was pretty sure I was going to look stupid.

I thought again of Conner's lame remark, and tried to shrug the feeling off.

In moments Conner was hovering above me. "Ready?" he asked.

"Sure." I took his hand, watching Jordan ascend the stairs from the corner of my eye. Today, I noticed that he'd covered the soles of his shoes with duct tape.

"Still talking to Jordan, huh?" he asked.

"Why not?" I countered, and surprisingly Conner was silent. We walked to class and he left me with a kiss. I looked in. Sure enough, these big guys were already in process, lifting weights.

There was a long bench nearby. I sat down by Mrs. Langston and a few others from P. E. class. "I'm glad you're here," she said. "We girls can lift too, you know."

I wasn't so sure. As I watched the guys lifting, it occurred to me that many of them had been lifting for some time, at least since the beginning of school year, and I really couldn't see the point in girls lifting weights. Looking at frog guts was one thing; weight lifting was another.

I watched as a guy lifted a huge weight the size of a truck tire. He didn't even groan. I was suddenly struck by his godlike beauty – sort of like Hercules – and tried to look away, but it was too late.

"Hey, you," he said, staring directly at me. "Want to be next?"

Mrs. Langston patted my shoulder. "Go ahead," she said.

I stood, my legs shaking. The feeling was sort of like the first time I'd had to give a book report in elementary school in front of the class, and sort of like the feeling I had right before kissing Conner for the first time. I don't know how I made it to the bench.

"I'm Chad," he said, reaching out his hand to shake mine. He was all sweaty in places I'd rather not mention, and his hand was warm.

"Brianne," I said.

"Well, Brianne, let me show you how it's done."

"You'd better change the weights first," I said.

"Right."

I watched a bit unnerved as Chad changed the weights out for some about the size of a large doughnut. "Two pounds," he said, grinning over at me.

He showed me how to lie on the bench, and where to put my hands. I could smell his sweat, all sour and rancid, and tried to think of something else when he leaned closer to me and worked my hands a bit.

"Now, squeeze your shoulder blades together."

"What?" I was so embarrassed I couldn't stand it.

"And raise your chest."

"My what?"

"Your chest." He blushed suddenly and I wanted to die.

"Tighten your upper back and keep your pinkies inside the ring marks."

"What?"

He pointed. "Your feet need to be flat on the floor."

"Got it," I said, feeling as stupid as ever.

"Straighten your arms so that you can lift the bar from the uprights."

"I don't…"

"You can do it. Just think of it as dissecting a frog."

I looked at him, my mouth wide open. "Why did you say that?"

"You like dissecting frogs. Most girls don't. Just think of lifting weights as doing something you like."

I thought of the chloroform smell and looked again at Chad's underarms. "Got it," I said.

"Now, move it until it's balanced over your shoulders."

Surprisingly, I managed this feat, though I felt the instant pressure of the weights bearing down on me, and in moments had replaced the bar.

"Done!" Chad said, reaching for me. I took his sweaty hand and he lifted me up. "Oscar would be proud of you, but be careful of Jordan, will you?"

I could do nothing but stare at him until the next victim came over to lift the weights. But when I was sitting down, a new thought struck me; and it was so far out there in la-la land I wondered if I'd ever make it back to reality.

What seemed like hours later, I was showering and getting ready for choir. Conner met me once more and walked me to class and when he was gone, I could think of little else. History was a fog and by the time school was over and I met up with Jordan Elspie, the words I'd had in my throat for a little over two hours, poured from my lips.

"Are all guys required to take weight lifting?" I asked.

Jordan blushed. We were sitting by the tree on our coats.

"No, why do you ask?"

"Well, I've been thinking about Audrey's killer," I said. "And it occurs to me that as long as the killer was in good shape, he could be any age, old or young."

"But he wouldn't necessarily have big feet."

He'd probably meant it as a joke, but I didn't laugh.

"My dad is in the hospital," I said.

"I know. You told me."

"And he's pretty strong, you know? But not now."

"When will he get out?"

It felt like a jail sentence sort of question but I ignored it. "Maybe a week. Maybe longer. He's still hooked up. He's awake and all that now, but he's still hooked up."

"How's your mom doing?"

"Okay, I guess. She cries a lot at home, and she seems to be distracted, but otherwise she's okay."

"Sounds sort of bad," Jordan said, shifting his feet in the snow.

"You know, I could get you some new shoes," I said.

"Conner told you."

"Yeah, but that's not why I want to get you some new shoes. Look at that tape, it's coming off."

"I know." He shrugged. Dad isn't around much, and the money is a bit tight."

I looked at his shoes again, thinking about what Chad had told me. But I couldn't believe he was warning me about Jordan too. "Let me get you some new shoes. We can figure stuff out about the case at the same time."

"You mean the killer's shoes?"

I nodded.

"I thought you already had the answer to that."

"Well, yes and no. I'm pretty convinced that they're Northway, but what color? I mean, wouldn't it be great to know that?"

"I don't know why. What does it matter the color of the killer's shoes?"

I couldn't believe Jordan couldn't see it. "The killer was driving an old car with bald tires, or maybe a new car with bald tires, but that doesn't make sense. If I had a new car I would have new tires on it. And so, if the killer has an old car, how can he afford to buy new Northways?"

"He saved money on the car?"

I couldn't help it. I laughed.

"Maybe he stole them?" Jordan quickly added.

"Maybe. But what if they weren't new Northways? Like in the sense that they had just come out? What if the Northways were used or were an old style and were on sale cheap enough for the killer to afford them?"

"All right, that makes sense. But I still don't get why we'd have to know the color."

"Colors come and go. So do styles; but when I buy shoes, there's always the popular colors of the year, and the old colors; the stuff that isn't so popular. If we checked out enough local stores, we might be able to find out what Northway shoes were sold in the clearance aisle after the summer, and from that list we could narrow down the color of shoes the killer might have been wearing. And then…"

"If we found the right color, we could pin the killer down!"

"Exactly!"

"And nothing is too much work for Audrey," Jordan said, standing.

After checking out numerous stores with Jordan, we finally reached the last one on the edge of town. All the salespeople before this last stop had looked at us strangely, and most of them hadn't really answered our questions, though we did find out that the killer's shoes might have been fluorescent yellow and black. That was the latest summer color according to Mark, the salesman at the latest shop. Of course, many of the shoes were carry-overs from the previous years, but there were only a handful of those in weird sizes, the biggest being a size 14.

"How big did you say the killer's feet were?" Jordan had asked, as we'd fished through the shoes. "Size 10 or thereabouts," I'd told him, bringing up blue colored one with white stripes.

"How can you be sure the killer wore a size 10?"

"I can't. Not really. I took a photo but it's at the police station." Anyway, I wear a size 7 in ladies and I know guys' sizes are a little different, but my dad wears a 10½. A bit of comparison helps."

"Why didn't you tell me that before?" Jordan lifted another shoe. It was red this time with no stripes. "Size 9," he said.

"I guess I didn't think of it. Sorry. I've been sifting through those photos for so long now; I almost have them imprinted in my head. What else would you like to know?"

We left the store and headed to the final one. It was a small shop connected to a bakery, like that made sense, but maybe people ate doughnuts while they were shopping for shoes.

"You know that weight lifting class I had to go to today?"

Jordan nodded and got in on the passenger side. He didn't have a car and that was fine with me. I was still using Dad's and wondered if he'd be using it again anytime soon. Anyway, I didn't mind driving. I turned on the heat and put the car in reverse.

"It was embarrassing," I said to Jordan." I mean, I could only lift small weights, and this guy, Chad, seemed to know it all. He even knew I liked dissecting frogs."

Jordan grinned over at me. "You do?" he said.

"Of course; I'm not just some lame girl."

"I know that. So how did he know you liked dissection?"

The thought had never crossed my mind. "You know what? This Chad even knew my brother. Do you think that's strange?"

"Maybe not; he is Conner's half-brother."

"What?" I couldn't believe it. I knew Conner had a twin sister but a half-brother? Why hadn't Conner ever said anything?

"They don't live in the same house but they have the same rotten Dad. But I understand all about rotten Dads."

"So, Conner's father remarried?"

"No, dummy, but Chad is the same age as Conner."

"Oh," I said, knowing what that meant, but not really wanting to reflect on it. And then I remembered. Months ago, at the dinner table, hadn't Oscar said something about having a friend named Chad?

"What do you know about him?" I asked.

Jordan paled. "Not much. I just know that Chad is as scary as his brother."

"So, why didn't you warn me about him?"

Jordan shrugged." I don't know. You're not dating him too, are you?"

I wondered why that mattered, but said nothing.

We stopped at the store, got out, and Jordan opened the glass door. We walked inside. A tall girl, about the size and width of a fence post, stared over at us. "Can I help you?" she asked, fingering the laces near the register. There was even a pair of tie-dyed ones. I showed them to Jordan.

"How long have you had these?" I asked.

"Oh, awhile now; not too many sales - oh, I guess I shouldn't have told you that." The girl blushed slightly and peered over at Jordan." I know you," she said. "Are you in my Chemistry class?"

Jordan shrugged. "Maybe," he said.

"You *are* in my chemistry class! Jordan, right?"

Jordan looked uncomfortable. He fingered the shoelaces on the rack and pulled off the tie-dyed laces for closer inspection – as if the laces needed closer inspection.

"Do you remember who bought the laces?" he mumbled, still staring down at them.

"Oh, how am I supposed to remember that?"

"Well, do you?" I asked. Actually, Jordan had presented a pretty good question. I'd discovered where the keychain had been purchased and who had purchased it by snooping around. Maybe Jordan was on to something.

"I don't know. Why do you need to know?"

"Remember that girl who was found dead in the park this winter?"

"Oh, her?" The salesgirl blanched. I couldn't see a name tag.

"So, you remember the girl from the paper?"

"Why, sure." She appeared younger than me and had a difficult time looking into my eyes, though there seemed to be no problem as she looked at Jordan. "I avoided Montgomery Park like the plague after I heard about her murder."

"Did you know her?" Jordan asked, placing the laces back on the display. He finally had the courage to look up.

"No, not really. But she came in here once or twice. When I found out she'd died, been murdered, it really gave me the creeps."

Jordan was intent now, and so was I. His fears suddenly evaporated at the prospect of learning more about Audrey Wilkins' murder.

"The second time I saw her she came in with this cute guy. Only…"

We waited, and I was about to speak when she continued: "At first, I thought he was cute. Tall. Black hair. But then, when she was down the aisle, he looked over at me, peered into my very soul. I didn't like it."

"Did he say anything to you?" I asked.

"No, just looked inside my brain."

"So, I guess you didn't know him."

"No. I mean, I knew *of* him, but we'd never really talked."

"What was his name?" Jordan asked.

129

"No idea."

"You didn't ask?"

"Oh, no. At least not after him staring at me like that."

"What happened then?" I asked.

"Nothing much, well, except they bought some shoes – for her. Kobear's. Bright red. And at the last minute, she grabbed for the tie-dyed laces."

I thought my heart would stop. "When was this?" I asked.

"Oh, just a few weeks before she was found dead; I couldn't believe it. I wondered how long it would take the cops to come over here and ask me tons of questions, but that never happened. You two are the first."

"What did the guy look like, other than having black hair and being tall?" Jordan asked. Someone else had entered the store. I looked back; a young boy with his mother.

"Welcome," the salesgirl said. "How may I help you?"

"We're looking for some school shoes, size 2," she said.

"Let me show you." The salesgirl left them both without another word and directed the woman and boy down the second aisle.

I looked over at Jordan, my heart pumping. "This is it," I said. "If we can get a full description of the guy who was with Audrey, we may have her killer."

Jordan was still. He looked into my eyes and I saw in them for the very first time – real fear. "What will we do after that?" he asked, placing his hands on my shoulders.

"Get you some shoes," I said. "You really need them."

Jordan smiled, revealing his yellow teeth, his foul-smelling breath funneling into my nose. But I tried to ignore it, and as the salesgirl returned she reached out her hand to Jordan. "My name's Kimberly," she said.

Jordan reached out his hand. "Pleased to meet you; this is Brianne."

"Hi. So, what about the guy with Audrey that day?" I asked.

"Oh. Well, he had dark hair, and had, ah… brown or hazel eyes or something like that. He was big, you know." She looked over at Jordan and blushed. "Not that all guys have to be big to be cute," she added, blushing again.

"What size were his feet?"

Kimberly laughed." I have no idea. They bought shoes for her I think. Maybe for him too, I can't remember."

"Right. So, what size do you think he wore?" I asked.

"Oh, I don't know. I really didn't look. But usually, the big guys have fairly large feet. My mom tells me they have to – you know, to hold their body up."

"What?"

"You know, so the person doesn't fall over. If they had small feet, they wouldn't be able to hold up their body."

"Right." Jordan stared at her, and she realized what Kimberly's comments had done to her brain, if only for a moment.

"Was Audrey wearing a tie-dyed sweat shirt when she came in?"

"No, I don't think so. I would remember that."

"And a scarf. Was she wearing a scarf?"

"Not that I remember. Why do you ask?"

"There was a scarf found around Audrey's neck when she was found dead."

"No – wait. She wasn't wearing a scarf but he was. It was a thick thing, red. I didn't think guys liked to wear scarves. I mean, I see so many not even wearing coats to school. You know? He was wearing this coat. I liked it because it matched his shoes. It may have been the new ones, but maybe not. I just knew that she bought new red ones to go with the laces. That I remember. But his... now that I think about it, they were probably not new, but not as old as yours," she added, looking down at Jordan's feet. "But old."

Jordan blushed.

"That's the other reason we've come in today," I said. "For Jordan."

"Want me to show you where they are?" Kimberly asked.

132

I nodded. We could ask follow-up questions down the aisle.

"Right here." Kimberly pointed to the section on row four. "I'm guessing you're about a size 7," she said.

"Eight," he squeaked, looking away from her eyes. So, he liked her. Now, that was something to remember.

"Right here."

Jordan started looking, and I couldn't help but smile. I wondered when he'd had a new pair of shoes, wondered how poor he really was, wondered about a lot of things I didn't understand.

Turning to Kimberly I asked, "So, do you remember what color shoes the guy wore?"

"Oh, no – wait. I think I can. They were one of our close-outs. Fluorescent yellow. And, ah, black."

"Air Mine 95s?"

"Right. I think that's right. How did you know that?"

I shrugged. I didn't know what else to do.

Jordan stopped, a box in his hands. "You still remembered a lot. Thanks."

"I do work in the shoe business," Kimberly said, her eyes blinking brightly. She was not only tall, but had thin legs. She was taller than Jordan, but this didn't appear to bother her.

"Oh, sure," Jordan replied.

"What size?" I asked, turning the conversation back to the yellow and black shoes.

"Now, that's something I'd have to look up. Just a sec."

She left us, and I wandered over to Jordan who had a pair of black running shoes. *New Balance*. I'd never heard of the brand before. They were only $25. "Is that really what you want?" I asked.

"These are great; besides, you don't need to spend a lot of money on me." He sat on the small stool with glass on one end for checking out feet, pulled off his old shoes – his socks were almost black, though I was sure they'd once been white – and placed the first shoe on his foot.

"Amazing!" he said, slipping on the other one and walking around. "I've never had a girl buy me anything before," he said, "well, except for the keychain from Audrey."

"Not even your mom?"

He frowned. "No. She died right after I was born."

I'd spoken before thinking and I felt bad. Still, Jordan seemed to be taking my words in stride. He was walking up and down the aisle as if he were the Prince of England. Finally, he stopped right in front of me and gave me a hug. "Can I wear them out?" he asked, his hazel eyes glistening.

"You mean out of the store?"

He laughed. "I'll probably wear them out, too."

He grabbed the old shoes, placed them in the box, and together we walked to the cash register where Kimberly was standing.

"Oh, you found some," she said, looking up. "And I have some good news for you. Size 11."

Shapes and Sizes

"So, I was off a bit," I said, getting into the car.

"No big deal. At least now we know. Size 11. That's pretty big."

"So, that would make the killer pretty tall, according to Kimberly."

"What do you think about her?"

"She seems nice, but I'm just going to have to forget about her."

"Why is that?" I asked. I was feeling hopeful for Jordan – hopeful that maybe he had found someone after losing Audrey.

"I already love someone else," he said, not looking at me.

I had a strange sensation crawl up my back, sort of like a lizard with claws. I wondered who he loved now, now that his dear Audrey was gone, but for some reason I couldn't bring myself to ask him.

I pulled out from the parking lot and headed for home. I had no idea where to take Jordan. The skies were getting dark and it wouldn't be long now before they'd be pitch black. I wondered if I should invite him over to the house. I wondered a lot of things I didn't say. We passed the school.

"Stop. Turn back."

"At the school?"

"Yep."

I turned the car around and Jordan directed me into the parking lot. "Over there," he said, waving.

Over there was nothing. Just an old shed of some kind attached to a relocatable – one of those make-shift houses that were built on school property for classes when the school couldn't hold all of the students.

I stopped the car in front of the relocatable and Jordan got out. "Thanks!" he said, coming around briefly to my door. I opened it slightly and the windows fogged up.

"Thanks again for the shoes." He reached his hand in and took mine. It was already cold.

"You live – here?"

Jordan smiled. "Not here, exactly. We sleep lots of places. This is just the perfect place for now."

"What about the heat?"

"It's heated. We just make sure the heater is turned off about two hours before school starts. That way no one knows we've been in here."

I couldn't believe it. "What about food?" I asked.

"Don't worry. My dad usually scrounges some up during the day while I'm at school. We'll have something."

I was sick. "Are you sure? I mean, I can drop by here later with something. I live just a few blocks…"

"I know, but don't worry about it. You've already spent enough on me."

I looked at Jordan's coat in the darkness. It looked *worn* even now.

***

Returning home, I found a letter in the screen door. Pulling it out, I brought it inside, turned on the light and removed my coat. It was almost seven.

"So, there you are," Mom said, coming into the room.

"Sorry, Mom."

I opened the closet and hung up my coat. I could feel my mom's eyes glaring through my back. I looked at the envelope briefly. It was from Conner.

I stuffed the envelope into my coat pocket and turned from the closet. My mom just didn't get it. I had my own life, things to do. Why couldn't she see that?

"Why didn't you call?"

So, that was it. "I forgot, but I do have some good news."

Mom reached for me, taking me into a warm hug. "I'm so glad you're here. I was worried about you."

Worried was an understatement, at least when it came to my mom, but I hugged her back." I was just out with Jordan."

"Jordan. Who's that?"

"A guy… from school."

"Oh. So, where has Conner Ryan been keeping himself these days?"

I'd more than likely opened up a can of worms, but I answered my mom anyway." I still see him. It's just, well, Jordan is much better at sleuthing."

"What have you found out?"

Mom sat on the couch and directed me to the other side. I looked into the kitchen briefly. Everything had been cleared off the table. "You've had dinner?"

"An hour ago; sorry you missed it."

"Me too."

"I'll fix you something in a minute. What did you find out?"

"The killer's shoe size."

Mom hesitated for only a moment." I thought you already knew that."

"I was just guessing, but now I have proof; Size 11. I also know the color. Yellow and black. Seems the guy paid cash so I don't have a name, but the salesgirl, Kimberly, gave us a great description of the killer."

"Wow."

My mom seemed sufficiently impressed. "Perhaps we should inform the police."

"Probably."

Mom grinned. "Now, you know what kind of trouble we've gotten into before when we haven't informed them."

"I know. It's just... Mom, I want to figure this one out by myself. If I had a name, then I'd go to the police. Right now, I just have a description. That can't mean much."

"You're wrong about that. When was the last time you watched a police show?"

I laughed." I guess I'm just trying to get out of telling them," I said.

"So, tell me about the killer," Mom said.

***

Conner was staring at me from the other side of the table. "Where have you been?" he asked. I could smell chloroform again. Today, we were dissecting a chicken. I looked down at the carcass, wondering how the guts would look this time.

"Sleuthing," I said, scalpel in hand. I looked down at the blade and twirled the knife in my hand. It was small, about the size of an emery board for nails, only longer. And it was silver. The thing could have never been used for killing anyone – or could it?

"Do they make these blades differently? I mean, does a dissecting blade differ from one a surgeon would use?" I asked.

Conner blinked over at me, his brown eyes surprised. "Yeah, sure. Probably."

"Do you think Mr. Jepson has one?"

"Why do you care about that?"

"Audrey Wilkins was killed with a knife, why not a scalpel?"

Conner blanched." I guess it's possible," he said.

"Have you ever owned any yellow and black shoes?" I asked, hoping to take Conner off guard.

He blinked over at me. "Sure, why do you ask?"

I couldn't believe it, but then again, I could.

"How come you don't wear them to school?" I asked.

"Oh, I haven't been able to find them." Conner looked into my eyes. "Why do you care anyway?"

"No reason, I guess."

Conner touched my hand from across the table. "Actually, I've looked for them. They were, well… anyway, I couldn't find them. After a few days, I just gave up."

"Oh, how long ago specifically?"

"Heck, I don't know." He turned away from me and let go of my hand." I bought them on sale… I probably shouldn't have but…" His voice trailed off.

"But what?"

"It doesn't matter," he said, not turning.

I thought about Conner with Audrey Wilkins, wondered about their friendship, because it had to have been a friendship, right? I couldn't bring myself to ask him anything else.

***

After class, and after the chicken beast had been dissected, I went up to talk to Mr. Jepson. Janine Wilks, who *also* shared my history class, and sat at the table closest to Mr. Jepson, looked over at me. "Like the chicken?" she cackled.

I nodded. "It was pretty cool," I said.

"I can still smell it," she said.

"The chloroform?" I asked.

"The dead chicken," she replied." I don't know how you do it." She picked up her books and left me without another word.

She was right, of course. I didn't know how I did it either, but the idea of figuring things out had always been on my list of favorites. I looked up at Mr. Jepson. He was putting some papers inside his desk drawer.

"Yes, Brianne?" he asked.

"I have a question."

I could hear the class leaving behind me, including Conner who had decided not to walk me to math. Things were changing and I wasn't sure how I was going to adjust.

"Shoot."

"Tell me about the scalpels. I mean, the one we use here is pretty small, but I hear you can get different ones."

"Why, sure," Mr. Jepson said, pushing the desk drawer shut. He walked around the desk to face me. "There are about as many scalpel sizes as there are types of people. Surgical blades, for example, can be shaped differently, depending on the procedure the doctor is doing. And when a person dies, morticians use a pretty strong blade."

"Cool," I said. "You don't happen to have blades like that that I could look at."

"Sure, but I keep them under lock and key."

I tried to breathe evenly as Mr. Jepson fished for the keys in his coat pocket." I used to keep them out, just during class, but the school didn't like that – too dangerous, they said, which is understandable." He pushed the key in the lock and opened the cupboard door just right of the sink. I'd never seen inside the cupboard before, though I'd had plenty of opportunities to see inside the others throughout the year. In it there was an old prop volcano, a vintage microscope, brass and all, and some apothecary jars with specimens inside. Mr. Jepson retrieved an old Cherry wood box about 7 or 8 inches long and unhooked the silver clasps.

Opening the lid, he looked in.

I followed suit.

But Mr. Jepson was silent. "I'm missing a blade," he said, looking over at me.

"What?" I asked, looking closer. Inside the wooden case were two pair of scissors and two scalpels – the space for a third scalpel was empty. "Wow," I said.

"Wow is right," Mr. Jepson echoed. "Last year, when they had me put away this thing, all the blades were here."

I took a deep breath and asked, "Do you think a person could be stabbed in the back with a blade like that?"

Mr. Jepson paled. "Sure. I mean, it happened in one horror movie I know of."

I looked inside the case one last time and Mr. Jepson shut it, hooking the silver clasps. Placing the box inside the cupboard he shut the door and locked it.

"When was the last time you saw the scalpel?" I asked.

Mr. Jepson was silent." I haven't gotten the case out at all this year. Not until now anyway. Last year, I brought the case home for the summer, and then I returned it to the shelf at the beginning of the school year. I didn't think to check inside. I live alone, and had no reason to expect that anything was missing."

Mr. Jepson looked into my eyes." I hope no one from this class has taken it," he said.

I was silent, my thoughts playing havoc with my brain. I could hear my heart beating strongly in my chest. The police, they'd never found the weapon as far as I knew. Nothing had been in the paper about it, nothing but a generalization of the murder weapon. Still, Officer

Hybrid had asked me if I'd seen the murder weapon, I did remember that.

"I'd better get to the office." Mr. Jepson looked into my eyes one last time. "And you'd better get to your next class."

Sleuthing

Something like paper was crumpled in my coat pocket. I pulled it out. The note! I'd forgotten all about it! Tearing up the now mangled envelope I pulled out the card. On the inside was a heart. I opened it.

"Dear Brianne,

Do you know how much you mean to me? I would be lost without you. I love you, do you know that? Please, let's forget the past and move forward.

Love, Conner."

I placed the card back into the envelope and shoved it into my backpack.

No wonder Conner had been so weird around me. I hadn't said anything about receiving the card! He must have thought I was completely nuts!

I thought back to a day ago, when I'd asked Mr. Jepson about the scalpel and before that, how strangely Conner had looked at me when discussing it and his yellow and black shoes. He had been waiting for me to say something. No wonder he'd left me and not walked me to Mrs. Wang's class.

When I reached my science class, Mr. Jepson pulled me aside. "Can we talk?" he asked. I looked over to my table. Conner hadn't arrived yet.

"Sure," I said.

Mr. Jepson walked me back out to the hall.

"I've been worried about that scalpel since yesterday," he began.

As students rushed by us, he lowered his voice." I have looked for it everywhere. This morning, I went and talked to Principal Gordon. He advised me to talk to the class about it."

"Do you think anyone will fess up?" I asked.

"That's what I'm hoping, but I need your help. Yesterday, you said something about using a scalpel for someone's death. I figured you were asking because of that girl, Audrey, that I'd read about in the paper."

"Wilkins," I said. "Her name was Audrey Wilkins."

"Yes. I also know you. I'm going to assume that you're right, but even if you're not, we need to find that scalpel."

"What do you want me to do?"

Mr. Jepson leaned in. I could smell his spearmint gum." I want you to watch the faces of the class when I tell them what is missing and tell me if you see or hear anything."

147

"Like what?"

"You know, a strange look. Someone whispering."

"Do you think the killer will reveal himself?"

"I didn't say we had a killer in the room. I'm just saying to watch. Maybe the person will admit they stole the scalpel. I'm going to offer a reward."

"How much?" I asked.

"$200."

"Wow," I said. "Is it really worth that much?"

"Probably not. But I want it to be enough."

The bell rang and Mr. Jepson stood straight. He looked into the classroom. With all of the whispering I hadn't been paying attention. Conner Ryan was already seated." I think it's plenty," I said.

I walked to my seat and sat down. "HI!" I said to Conner. He ignored me.

Mr. Jepson stood before the class." I have a request of you," he began, his eyes searching the room. "One I hope you can help me with."

I didn't look at Conner, but I could smell his aftershave. I could feel his eyes. He was staring at me.

"I am offering a $200 reward…"

There was a collective gasp in the room not unlike the sound of a waterfall tumbling.

"…I am missing one of my priceless scalpels from this case." He held up the Cherry wood case for the class to see. Yesterday, I opened it to discover that one of my scalpels was missing."

"Where did you have it last?" Janine Wilkes asked. Conner Ryan shifted in his chair but I kept my eyes on the class.

"In this case. See this key? I use it to lock up the cabinet."

"So, what you're saying is that someone broke into the cabinet and stole your priceless item."

"Could be. Or, I might have used it in class one day to help a student with their project."

Conner breathed in and raised his hand. "What does it look like?"

"Like a scalpel, dummy."

I looked around the class but couldn't tell who had spoken.

Mr. Jepson continued: "Actually, the scalpel is used for anatomy. It was given to me by my grandfather who worked as a mortician. As you can see there are two scissors and two scalpels currently in the case. I am missing the largest one that looked similar to the ones here." Mr. Jepson handed the case to Janine. She pecked inside briefly and passed it on.

By the time the case had reached me and Conner, there was silence in the room like a morgue – no one was speaking. I looked inside the case, closer this time, and could smell the faint scent of wood. Conner touched me on the shoulder. "You must have seen this yesterday," he said.

I nodded, stood and returned the case to Mr. Jepson.

"If you find the instrument, please let me know as soon as possible. Remember the reward is $200."

"I wish I had it," Conner said, taking my hand but I just couldn't look into his eyes.

"I'm sorry about not thanking you for the note."

"I was wondering about that."

I looked up then. "I'm really sorry," I said.

"No problem." He caressed my hand. "You have been pretty busy."

My heart thumped, as it always did when Conner was especially near, but I tried not to glue my eyes to him. I'd listened like Mr. Jepson had asked me to. I'd watched faces and eyes. And other than Conner's comment about wishing he had it, I hadn't noticed anything out of the ordinary.

***

"I'll get it!" Someone was knocking on the door, and the knock was pretty insistent. I looked through the peep hole. Green eyes stared back at me.

"Emily?" I said, opening the door. "Emily Ryan?"

"Hi, Brianne. Can we talk?"

I had the strangest sensation crawl up my back, like a cockroach, but it was a feeling I was beginning to recognize as important. "Come on in."

Emily brushed by." I bet you were expecting my brother," she said.

Actually, I was – In just about an hour or so.

"He'll be by. I just needed to talk to you before that." Emily brushed the dark hair from her eyes and tried to smile over at me. We were sitting on the couch, and she was facing me. But I couldn't get over the feeling I had, not only about her being here in the first place, but about what she wasn't yet saying that I could already feel coming from her green eyes.

"You need to stay away from my brother." Her eyes were suddenly bugging out at me, and all I could think about was a dead frog lying before me all ready to be dissected.

"What?" I croaked.

"Look. Don't get mad. It's just…" Emily rolled her eyes and stared me down. "It isn't – safe."

"This is your brother we're talking about."

"I know. But I want you to trust me. Can you do that?"

Amazingly, though I'd seen Emily in the halls between classes, and we'd had no classes together this year, I felt like I should trust her. The thing with Conner had to be pretty important for her to come to me now.

"Okay, I guess. But he's going to be here in less than an hour."

"I know. I want you to be gone. Can you do that?"

It was the strangest request, but not as strange as some of the other things I'd done as part of my sleuthing.

Emily stood. "Thanks. I'll see myself out."

I watched her walk to the door, tighten her coat around her and leave me. After she'd gone, I told Mom I was leaving to do some errands, went to the closet, took out my coat, and walked out to my dad's car. I got inside and drove over to Jordan's place. On my way, I thought about the words Emily had used – sort of grown-up words. Who said, 'I'll see myself out,' except for old people?

I drove up to Jordan's shack behind the school and knocked on the door. That's when it occurred to me. Maybe my mom wasn't safe either. I had no idea where Oscar was. How could I leave them like that?

As I stood in front of the door, my coat wrapped around me snuggly, gloves on my hands and a hat on my head to keep the extra chill off, I knocked again.

No one came.

Just as well. Getting in the car I returned home, only to find Conner standing inside. My mom was offering him some hot cocoa. He looked up when he saw me, and his brown eyes said all.

"Sorry," I began, taking my coat off and stumbling to the couch. Sitting across from him, I watched as he took a sip. "I had something to do."

The warning words of Emily ran frantically within my mind. I turned to my mom. "You can sit with us," I said.

Mom looked at me in surprise. "I'll leave you two alone."

"No! I mean, you've always said you wanted to get to know Conner better."

Actually, my mom had never really said that, only inferred it a couple of times. I couldn't help it. I was scared out of my wits. It was almost as if Conner was yelling at me as he sipped that cocoa – as if words passed between us – unspoken words that were feeling their way into my flesh. I'd known Conner for months now, and with one word from his sister I was scared to death.

And then I remembered. Jordan had also warned me.

"So?"

Conner sat his cup down and waved me over.

I didn't move.

"What's wrong with you?" he asked.

"Nothing – nothing."

"No, really? Did you forget our date or something?"

"No. I mean, yes, I mean, I don't know."

"Come here." He prodded me with his hand. "You're so far away."

I slid across the couch towards him. Sitting next to him, I forced my breathing to slow down. I tried not to think of the warnings I'd received, and then it occurred to me, my brother had also warned me.

Conner placed his arm around me. "I'm worried about you," he said.

His words sounded so genuine, so full of love.

"I'm sorry I wasn't here," I said.

"Where were you?"

"I… was looking for Jordan."

Conner tensed up. "What do you see in that guy anyway? Are you dating him or something?"

"No. Heck, Conner, why are you so jealous? He's a friend, just a friend!"

"Whoa, whoa, where is this coming from?"

I turned my eyes up to him; a tear dropped.

"You're shaking. Are you cold or something?"

I couldn't believe it. I couldn't believe we were sitting together and that for the first time I was utterly and completely afraid. Where had the love gone? The desire for him to be close to me?

"I'm scared of you, that's what!" I yelled.

"What?" Conner's arm dropped from around me. He stood and bore his eyes into mine. "Why would you be afraid of me? I've never hurt you!"

"You do get angry sometimes."

"And you don't?" He was pacing now, his eyes heated. Maybe my mom would walk in. Maybe Oscar would come home. "Who have you been talking to?"

"W-what?"

"Talking to?" Conner looked down the hall and lowered his voice. "Who has told you to stay away from me?"

So, he knew.

"No one…"

"Liar." The venom in his words hissed.

I was more afraid in that moment than I'd ever been. He was a raging lion above me and all I could do was cower. Where was my mom? Anyone?

"Calm down," I whispered.

"What did you say?"

"Calm down," I said a bit more loudly.

He smiled at me, but the smile I received didn't warm me. It said, *I am going to find out who's been talking to you about me and they're going to get it.*

Danger

It wasn't like Jordan not to attend school, but as one day grew into two and I didn't see him – art was a vacant lot without him there – I turned again to Oscar.

He was readying himself for something, combing his hair, when I decided to speak up.

"Conner's sister came to see me," I said.

"Oh?"

"Two days ago. She came to warn me about Conner."

Oscar stopped combing his hair and looked over at me. "Like I said."

"Why would she do that?"

"I don't know, but I'm already late. Can we talk about this later?"

"What have you got, a date?" I asked.

"No. A party."

It was Friday night and the last thing I wanted was for Oscar to get drunk or something. I needed him now, and I needed him to be sober.

"I need to talk to you." I hoped my words sounded insistent, demanding even. Oscar had to hear me out, he just had to."

"Shoot then," he said.

"Can you look at me?"

Oscar turned, dropping the comb on the counter. "Okay, I'm looking."

"Okay." I took in a deep breath. I'd been preparing my speech all day, hoping that I'd be able to find the right words without Oscar going on the defensive – he just couldn't go on the defensive. I needed him.

"Do you think Conner Ryan could kill anyone?"

Oscar's mouth dropped open." I don't know."

"You don't know?"

"Look. Maybe once he could have done that. In Jersey. But he seems a bit calmer now."

"Calmer?"

"Yes, calmer. Why, is that funny or something?"

"No," I said. "I have been doing some research on Audrey Wilkins. Have you seen Conner's yellow and black Northways, size 11?"

"What?" He looked at me quizzically. "Heck, how would I know? You're the one with him all of the time."

"Is he coming with you tonight?"

"Maybe."

"Oscar, I really need your help."

"To check out his shoes?"

"No, I mean, yes."

Conner laughed. "You're really going crazy, sis. Anything else I can do for you?"

"Um… ask him about me. See how he's feeling."

"Did you two get into a fight or something?"

"Sort of."

"Figures. He didn't hit you, did he?"

"No, he didn't hit me, but why are you so worried about that anyway?"

Oscar hesitated. "Just thinking about the girl from…"

"Who was it?"

"I don't know; just some girl."

"Do you know her name?"

"Does it really matter? In happened in Jersey."

"Oh."

"Look, Brianne. Like I said, you need to be careful about Conner, but not so careful you become some frenzied psycho."

"You told me to break up with him."

"No, I didn't."

"Yes, you did. And Jordan told me to do the same thing."

"Jordan who?"

"Jordan Elspie."

"Who's that?"

"A guy from my art class; he's helping me with the case."

Oscar looked at me intently, as if trying to see what I was thinking.

"So, this new guy... oh, I get it, Conner's jealous or something, right?"

"No."

"Right."

Oscar turned his back to me and picked up the comb.

"I'm really worried," I said, blinking at myself in the mirror. Oscar had shifted to the left and I could see myself in living color. It frightened me. I was as pale as milk or a sheet, or whatever a person said when they looked sick.

"Look, sis. What am I supposed to do? Ask Conner if he killed that girl?"

"Would you?"

Oscar plunked the comb on the counter and turned to me. "You're kidding, right?" He looked into my face, perhaps for the first time, and placed his hand on my shoulder. "Are you really worried about Conner, or are you trying to get him off your back so you can date this other guy?"

I couldn't believe it. I couldn't believe any of it. My brother wasn't the brightest light in the room but we'd grown up together. Didn't he understand anything?

"Can we sit on your bed?" I asked.

"Sure, but make it quick."

I wasn't sure if I could make my last words quick, but I rehearsed all of the things I'd spoken to my brother about before and added some new twists that he hadn't heard yet. I talked about my research, about the keychain found in the snowball, about the way the girl died, about everything that I could think of, and when I was done Oscar said, "Wow. You've really been working at this. And you say Mom and Dad are helping you out. How come I don't know anything?"

I shrugged, but I longed to tell my brother the truth. He was never home. He never sought me out to talk to me anymore. I was a stranger to him.

"I can see why you might think the killer is Conner. What did you say about the sun keychain?"

"It was gift from Audrey Wilkins to Jordan Elspie."

"And you say you found it and returned it to him?"

"He wanted it back, he…"

"That probably should have gone to the police. What do Mom and Dad say?"

I pushed my hand in my back pocket and pulled out the keychain Mom had bought me.

Oscar gasped. "Holy crap!" he exclaimed, though the word wasn't crap but a swearword I'd rather not repeat.

He grabbed the sun from my hands and held it up." I didn't think I'd ever see this thing again! He turned it over in his hands. "Where's the inscription?" he asked.

"There isn't one. I told you, this one is the one *Mom* bought for me."

"Oh, sorry."

"How did you know about the inscription?" I asked.

"You told me."

"No. I told you where I'd found the keychain, and who it belonged to. I didn't say anything about what was written on it."

Oscar paled. "OH," he said.

"You know something."

"Yes."

"Tell me."

Suddenly my brother looked sick." I don't know if I can."

"Why not?"

"I might throw up if I say it."

"It can't be that bad."

Oscar paced the room like there was no tomorrow. "You can't tell anyone," he began.

"Tell them what?" I countered.

I was still sitting on the bed, but my brother's words made me feel sick. What would he tell me? That he was somehow mixed up in the murder of Audrey Wilkins?

"Now, you've got to promise me that you won't tell Mom or Dad."

"I can't promise that."

Oscar turned from me. All I could see was his back. "You've got to."

If it was time for lying, this time was it. If I didn't agree to Oscar's request, I would never know the secret. And I had to know the secret.

"Okay, I promise."

Oscar turned. He wasn't smiling, in fact his face looked pained.

"I thought that keychain was gone for good. When Chad Ryan first showed it to me, and told me whom he'd stolen it from, I laughed. I can't believe I laughed, but I did. He showed me the inscription: Something about not being a morning person. He told me that the kid was a nut job. That it was about time he taught him a lesson."

"He told me the kid's name: Jordan. But until now, I hadn't connected the two."

"How does Chad know Jordan?" I asked.

"Evidently, they got into a fight at some park about some girl Jordan liked."

"What park?"

"I think it was Montgomery."

I felt sick. "Who was the girl?" I asked.

"That's the strange part. After getting heated about the keychain and telling me a lot about the fight – Chad easily won and sent Jordan home crying – he clammed up. I tried to bring it up numerous times after that but Chad wouldn't tell me a thing; he even pretended that I was making stuff up. It was like we'd never had the conversation. After a while, I quit asking him."

"Wow," I said.

"There's something else."

I held my breath, and then a thought came to me, a thought even more frightening than what I'd just heard." I met this Chad in the weight room."

"He told me."

"He knew all about the dissection stuff with Conner."

"Conner probably told him."

"He also told me to be careful about Conner."

"I warned you, too, remember?" He walked to the mirror. "Is that it?"

"So, what were they fighting about?" I asked.

"Like I said, some girl."

"One they both liked?" I asked, feeling a bit uncomfortable as my brother primped in front of the mirror.

"You know, that was the weird part. I don't think Chad liked her."

***

Though Dad had finally returned from the hospital, he still looked weak – and pale. I sat by his bed on one of the first nights he was home and we spoke about the case. I told him everything I dared to, including my conclusions about Conner Ryan, and my dad listened as if there was no tomorrow.

Perhaps there wasn't, at least not very many for my dad, but I tried not to think about that. Maybe we could come to some sort of conclusion who was the killer. Maybe my dad could help remove some of the cobwebs.

Those first few nights Mom joined us and we pieced together the case like a quilt. It was helpful to have feedback on the clues, even more helpful to know that many of my thoughts weren't as removed from sanity as I'd first thought.

"Things are really coming together," Dad said, scooting himself up farther on the bed. I grabbed for a second pillow and added it to the one he already had behind his back.

"Thanks."

"Maybe it's time to talk with the police again," Mom said.

I looked over at her. She had dark circles around her eyes and she looked tired. For days now I'd done my sleuthing alone. Without Jordan, things were getting done in half the time and I knew Mom had done little in the way of the case because of all of the problems with Dad's heart. I knew they loved each other; I also knew that because of that, there had been little time to think about the case.

"I guess I could tell them what I know; like they'll believe me."

Mom smiled. I knew enough about her experience with previous cases to know that few in the police department had believed her either until she'd proven them wrong.

164

What I knew for sure is that I needed to find Jordan Elspie. And I needed to talk to my brother again about Conner's half-brother, Chad.

Revelation

Mr. Cordial walked up to me. I was working on a new project, a watercolor, though my recent projects had gotten to him late and my grade would be docked by 10 percent. Focus was hard these days – about as difficult as finding Jordan Elspie. I missed him.

And so, it was no surprise when my teacher had the same concerns.

"How is your watercolor coming?" he asked first, peering down at it. "Nice," he added softly.

"It's not much – yet," I said, brushing the landscape in golden tones. It was the park, Montgomery Park, before the killing, before I'd started running, before I'd even met Jordan Elspie. I had a picture of the park which I'd enlarged next to me. The tree would come next.

"Have you seen Jordan lately?" he asked.

It had been a week and I hadn't.

"The address he gave the school is false; hasn't lived with the Ryans for over a year. Funny, his father met with me on occasion but he never said anything either."

"You mean Conner Ryan?"

"I've only spoken with the father. Who is Conner?"

"His son." I placed my brush in the can of water above the painting.

"I guess I should have said something," I said, looking into Mr. Cordial's eyes. They were blue. It was the first time I'd really noticed. I thought of my other teacher, Miss Meacham, the one he might yet be dating, but I only thought of her briefly. "Jordan's been living over at the relocatable behind the school."

Mr. Cordial blinked. "For how long?"

"Not sure, but it's pretty cold out and I imagine they needed somewhere to stay."

"How do you figure they got inside?"

"Jordan had a key to the place, I guess. He and his father vacated every morning before school started so that they wouldn't be caught."

"Still, I can't believe no one noticed."

"I can't believe I can't find his father even. Where do you think they might have gone?"

I thought of all the places that Jordan and I had visited during our sleuthing, but he wouldn't take his father to any of those places I was pretty sure – except maybe Montgomery Park. There wasn't much in terms of shelter there, however.

I shook my head." I have no idea, but I've been pretty worried about him too. I guess he's been homeless."

"I had no idea. So many things make sense now."

"Like what?" I asked.

"His clothing, his hygiene. He is a great student, don't get me wrong but I wanted to talk to him about some of those things, help him in some way."

I thought about the coat then, all ragged and worn.

"I'll keep my eyes out for him," I said, "and let you know if I see him."

Mr. Cordial left me and I peered down at my watercolor. I had forgotten the stream. That had to come first before the tree.

***

That day, after school was out, I went back to the park, mostly to think, but partly to see if there was any sign of Jordan Elspie. There wasn't.

It was mid-March, and the snows weren't near as thick as they'd been the day I'd found Audrey Wilkins, her hair frozen to the ground in some sort of sunrise motif. I thought about the girl's hair, about the keychain, and pulled the copy keychain out of my backpack before sitting down.

I loved the blue stone inside it. I loved how the rays reached out, as if reaching for the sky. Crouching by the tree, I touched its thick trunk, wondering about the secrets it held; what it could tell me if it could talk. Bare of leaves, it would soon push forth new growth, and before too much longer, the warmth of the sun's rays would filter through the leaves.

Blue. The stone was blue. Not yellow. Not orange. Not red.

I'd often thought of Jordan as separate, different, the sort of guy who kept to himself unless he felt comfortable. He had been outspoken about Conner, and that was strange, seeing as, before that, he'd never spoken to me at all.

His hazel eyes had spoken volumes to me after we'd gotten to know one another, and though he was only a sophomore, he was cute in his own way, and through the weeks I had grown quite attached to him. He was sort of like a puppy.

I thought about all of the times I'd wanted to ask him about Audrey, but hadn't. In all of his forthcoming information, he'd been pretty quiet about her and I wondered why that was. I should have asked more questions. I should have pushed him a little.

But it was too late now. Jordan was gone and I would probably never see him again.

A slight sound near the stream caught my attention. It was a bird, chirping in a bare tree overlooking the water. The bird was blue. I watched it for a moment, and turned back to the tree, sliding my fingers over the rough bark. Something was near the

169

bottom, carved almost at the tree's base, something small.

I had missed it before, because of the snow hiding much of the trunk, but now, the words jumped out at me like a lizard pouncing. *I'm not a morning person either*, it read. And it was signed: *Conner.*

My heart stopped. I looked closer, touching the carved writing with my finger. Reaching into my purse, I grabbed my phone and took a picture. And then I took another and another. The shot had to be perfect. I had to be able to read every letter.

Satisfied, I enlarged the picture. Yes, the name was definitely, *Conner*. I couldn't believe it. I couldn't believe what I'd found; an actual piece of evidence that connected Conner to the crime. Had he actually pushed the keychain into the snowball, and placed the ball by the tree near his carving? Was the scalpel the weapon used here, too?

Was Conner the killer?

I tried to breathe evenly but it was no use. I was too excited; too mortified. Could I be both? I'd kissed Conner numerous times. I'd held his hand. I had shared personal things with him, and all this time, he might have killed me just like he had Audrey Wilkins!

I stood, placing the keychain back in the pocket of my backpack, and my phone inside my purse. I hadn't been to the police yet with my most recent evidence before this lucky find today, but perhaps it was finally time.

***

Officer Hybrid stared at me, lifting his gray eyebrows.

"Where is this tree?"

"By the stream, like I said. I didn't see it before because it was covered with snow."

"We have been talking to Jordan Elspie," he said. I was surprised at the confession. It was the first. "He showed us the keychain." He looked closely at the photo on my phone. "The words on the tree trunk are hard to read."

I enlarged the picture for him. "See? And look, there's the signature."

Officer Hybrid peered closer." I think you're right," he said, handing me back my phone. "Who is Conner?" he asked.

"Conner Ryan. Do you know him?"

"We've spoken." The man blushed as if embarrassed. "Interesting, very interesting."

"Have you seen Jordan? He hasn't been to school in a week."

"No, but since you mention it, he has called us once or twice this past week." Officer Hybrid ruffled through the papers on the table. "Here it is. Looks like the last time he called was two days ago – something about being followed – that he had to get away."

"He was living at the relocatable at the school."

"Yes. Georgia Meacham at the school has been looking out for him."

"You mean the English teacher?"

"Sure. I thought you knew."

"No."

"When Jordan was kicked out of the Ryan place, she told me she had to do something. She felt bad about making a copy of the key to the relocatable, but said she just couldn't have one of her students sleeping out in the cold. She was worried she'd be locked up or something."

"For what, making a key?"

Officer Hybrid smiled. It was the first smile I'd ever seen coming from his face. It almost looked funny, but I tried to remain focused.

"The school doesn't even know. I told her that I'd keep her secret if she helped us with the case."

"She's not a detective…"

"Funny you should ask. We needed someone from the inside to scout out the goings-on of Jordan Elspie and that Conner Ryan."

"So, did he do it? Did Conner Ryan kill Audrey Wilkins? And if so, why?"

"Now, that's something I can't tell you for sure. Innocent before proven guilty, but I can tell you that, with the information you've just given us, it's more than the right time to revisit our conversation with Conner Ryan."

***

The next day at school, Conner didn't show up to science class. I didn't see him at lunch, and when the final class for the day, history, was behind me, I walked home alone, thinking of what Conner could be thinking of me now. Would the police say that I'd given them this last tidbit of information? Probably not. Still, what would Conner be like when I saw him again?

As the thoughts whirled inside me, I continued to walk alone. But I wasn't alone. You know that feeling you get when you can't see a person behind you, but you feel them matching your steps? Well, that was what it was like for me that day I walked home alone without Conner. I felt as if I was being followed.

I couldn't look back, but once I'd rounded the corner, I just couldn't help but look back. It was her. Yes. Janine Wilks. I stopped. "What do you want?" I asked.

She stopped a few feet from me and then continued as if I hadn't spoken. Walking up to me, and close enough that I felt uncomfortable, she said, "I can't believe you'd do that to Conner."

I took a deep breath, waiting for her cackle. It didn't come.

"I've been watching you and I can't believe you'd be so cruel."

"Watching me – when?"

"You must think I'm pretty stupid, the teacher's pet or something. But I know you. I know who you are and I know what you do."

"And what is that?"

"You're trying to implicate Conner in this thing."

I looked at Janine, really looked at her this time, and like the feeling I'd had with Officer Hybrid, I was suddenly noticing the girl's eyes – brown – just like the eyes of Audrey Wilkins. Just like the eyes of Conner." I love him, you know, and I would do anything to keep him safe."

Janine was tall, taller than I'd first thought her, whether it was in science or in history. I'd always thought her weak and weird, but now I was looking at her upper arms hidden beneath her coat. I was staring at her feet and what was on them.

Shoes. Yellow and black shoes.

Laces

As I looked down at the laces on Janine's feet, she said: "I have always loved Conner. He is the truest friend I have ever known."

I looked up. "Then you dated," I said.

"It was my dream. But sometimes, dreams just don't come true. Still…" She looked down at her shoes. "Some things can be…obtained." She reached her arm quickly around mine and held me close, "I do have my imagination. You know about imagination."

I tried to swallow. Scream. I could barely see my house, just there, about ten houses down.

"I would suggest you do as I say," she said.

I thought about Jordan then, wondered if he was all right, if Janine had already gotten to him, but Janine was taking me in the opposite direction, in the direction of the park.

Her arm held me strongly, and as I thought about the knife that was more than likely near her, I screamed – once – that was all, before her hand roughly found my mouth." I would advise you to listen to me. Quiet, or you will die here."

I looked up the street as I walked, hoping someone would come out of their house and retrieve their mail, get in their car, see me with Janine as we walked up the street together, but other than an occasional dog that barked, we were alone.

And then I saw it. The car. The car I was sure had gotten Conner so angry. There was a man inside. The man he'd more than likely fought with that night of the Valentine dance. I pulled Janine's hand from my lips. "Help!" I screamed, praying he would stop. I stomped on Janine's foot and ran towards that old car as if my life depended on it.

She let go of me with a wail and I rushed from her evil grip. "Help!" I screamed again, tromping through the snow, the ice, and who knows what else to get to him. Breathing heavily, I finally had to stop, the car was turning the corner anyway, and the man probably hadn't seen me.

And if he had?

Suddenly I was in Janine's falcon like grip. "What did I tell you?" she breathed, pushing me against her side and continuing to walk me to the park. "Silence!"

I blinked, stray tears falling down my cheeks. We walked through the slight snow until we'd reached the tree. Pushing me down at the foot of it, she hovered eerily above me. I looked down at her feet, now close enough that I could see that they were indeed Northways – Conner's Northways.

"I've been worried about you and Conner for some time," she began." I could see that you were getting close, too close. What is a friend to do?"

Janine squatted in front of me. I looked into her eyes but all I saw was hate.

"It's always the cute girls that get their man, but I could never understand why he picked you. You're more ordinary, like me, than the other girls he had his eyes on."

"You mean, like Audrey Wilkins," I said.

The smell of tobacco escaped her lips. "She was easy. So small. I couldn't understand what Conner saw in her. She was far too young for him."

"Maybe he didn't like her in that way," I said.

"What way?" Janine asked. Janine sat, taking my right hand roughly in hers. She held it tightly, like a vice.

"In a romantic way. You know."

"How was I supposed to know *how* he felt? Huh? He wasn't talking to me anymore. All I wanted was the truth, but he didn't have time for me."

I wanted to ask, *what truth?* But the words wouldn't come.

"It was easy to set everything up. Cause commotion."

"Where is he?" I asked.

"Who?"

"Jordan. Where is Jordan?"

177

"Who knows? So, tell me, how do you feel about Conner? I've seen you two kiss." She spit on the ground as if just the thought of it made her sick. "When I'm assured Conner will have nothing to do with you anymore, then we can get back to where we were."

Janine reached for a snowball. "Did you like the present?" she asked.

"So, it was you."

"Who else?"

"How did you get the keychain? I mean, it belongs to Jordan."

"How do I get anything? How did I get you?"

I shuddered. It was cold on the frozen earth, but I wasn't shuddering because of that. Janine had more than a creepy laugh about her as I was soon discovering. She had a creepy heart.

"Where is he?"

"After my interrogation. What do you think of the stream here?" she asked.

"I don't know."

"Come on, Brianne. Tell me."

"It's beautiful in the summer. I always – come here."

"Yes, I know. What else? Tell me about the tree."

"It's nice too. When did Conner write that saying on the tree anyway?" I'd suddenly, miraculously, found my voice.

"He didn't. I did. Let's see, day before yesterday."

"What?"

"I had to get you to implicate Conner, if only for a time. I was so mad at him. Had to pay him back – somehow. But now I see the truth. The past is the past, and all I have to look forward to is the future. I have it all worked out."

She smiled smugly, still gripping my hand.

"What if he doesn't love you?"

Janine's eyes burned.

"I do – love him. Much more than you could ever hope to. And he loved me. It was always so until Audrey got involved."

Why was it that the eyes always spoke volumes that nothing else would? Janine's eyes were not only brown, they were blood shot. She'd either been crying or was on something.

"Now, do you know what you need to do? Free me. Maybe yourself. Now, that would be a treat."

"You killed Audrey. Why?" I asked, my heart pumping in my chest.

"I told you. She was in the way."

"But it was only friendship!"

"I can't be certain of that and neither can you. Just be glad that your own precious life has been spared."

"So – you're not going to…"

"I could. I will if I have to."

"So, who do you'll pin the crime on? The police know about the keychain. They know about Jordan's friendship with Audrey. They spent a lot of time

179

together, but the other clues don't match up, you have to know that. Jordan's too small to have carried Audrey to the stream. His feet aren't large enough, unlike yours.

It was as if a sudden bolt of lightning reached forth its rays and touched Janine. She looked at me and laughed, the sound of the witch coming out in all its glory. "What clues. Tell me."

"The shoes for one. You're wearing them."

Audrey looked down and took the right shoe off. "You mean, these?" she said. "And these?" she added, fingering the tie-dyed laces." I had to do something to remember the event by. And it was surely – an event."

I felt sick.

"You're completely sure I was wearing them at the time?"

"What? I mean, sure I'm sure."

"And that I carried the corpse all the way to the tree here?"

"Yes."

"Why would I do that? Why would I bring Audrey Wilkins here?"

"Why wouldn't you? It's winter. Cold. No one is here."

"But you were here, weren't you Brianne. You were."

"Yes."

"It was easy getting the scalpel from Mr. Jepson's cabinet. Harder, was using it. I am pretty strong for a girl, but blood and gore, it was really never my favorite thing."

Janine stood, peering down at me again. "Conner would never look at me, you know. The friendship we had when we were younger no longer meant anything to him when Audrey came along. After she was gone, he found you. I could never believe the attention he gave you. I couldn't believe he wasn't afraid to be around you. But maybe, just maybe, he didn't want to be linked to the crime, and in some strange way, felt that in helping you out it would take your mind off what he was really capable of."

She laughed. "So, will you help me?"

"With what?"

"Well, we've got to blame someone for the crime.

"Who?"

"Jordan, of course."

"There's no way…"

"With the help of Chad."

I knew very little about Chad, only that he was the half-brother of Conner and had a great physique. I also knew that he'd gotten into a fight with Jordan – and won.

But I *knew* Jordan, and not only knew him, but liked him.

***

The girl was crazy. I could just go to the police whenever I wanted, once she left me. I would find Jordan and I would pretend to help, as if that really mattered. There was a screw loose, maybe five, in Janine's head.

Clutching my arm, she returned me to the school and pushed me in the direction of the relocatable. He's in there," she said.

"His father?"

"Dead. Go."

I couldn't believe the police weren't here, that someone wasn't at the school, hoping that father or son would return. But the place was as empty as a cemetery.

Janine unlocked the door. I didn't knock. I turned the knob. Jordan was sitting in the corner, chained to a desk.

He sobbed when he saw me. "I'm so sorry," he began, reaching for me. I held him like a child, my child.

"What happened?" I finally managed to ask.

Jordan wasn't even wearing a coat. The room was cold. Taking my own coat off I placed it around his shoulders.

"She wants me to confess," he said.

"I have other plans," I offered.

"But I have to confess. I was there," he said.

"There. Where?" I sounded like a Dr. Seuss rhyme but I didn't care.

"When Audrey died. In the parking lot. I'm so sorry, Brianne. I should have told you."

My heart was suddenly as frozen as the room. What was Jordan saying?

"They had it all planned out."

"Who?"

"Janine and Chad."

"What?"

"Listen. I have to do this. Janine is so angry. She said she'd kill you if I didn't confess."

"She doesn't like blood," I said. It was a funny thing to say, but something in our previous conversation had struck a nerve.

"I know. She doesn't do any of the dirty work anyway. Chad does."

"You mean he killed Audrey?"

"I think so."

"And Janine carried Audrey to the tree?"

Jordan nodded. He was sniffling now, and any moment I knew Janine would be pulling the two of us apart. Only she wasn't. I found it strange that she wasn't.

"So, why did you warn me about Conner?"

Jordan shifted uneasily on the floor, and opened and closed his fingers. I couldn't see any redness around his wrists.

"Janine likes him," he said." I didn't want you to get hurt."

I nodded and Jordan continued: That night, I wished he'd been there, but his brother was there instead, and Chad gets even angrier than his brother does."

I couldn't believe it, any of it, but I just had to. Jordan had seen something, something so terrible and yet so secretive that he hadn't been able to tell me until now.

"There was a fight that night. After Audrey…"

"Who was fighting?"

"Chad and our captor."

"Janine?"

"After they got rid of Audrey, they walked down the pathway together, yelling and screaming at each other. I followed them to the car. Janine was insistent about following Chad into the car, but he locked the car doors. I could hear her yelling from the outside, trying to pull the doors open. When Chad sped off, Janine stood there for a long time. In the cold. I was shivering myself and knew that I would be sick if I didn't hurry home."

I was more than confused now. How could Chad and Janine have been fighting near the stream? Wouldn't someone have heard them? And what about the footprints? There was only one set – that, I knew for sure.

"I need to confess. I was there. I didn't go to the police," Jordan said.

"But you didn't kill Audrey Wilkins. That has to mean something."

"Are you about finished?" Janine's words filtered through the cold air. She brushed by me and pulled Jordan up. He stood, wearily, trying to maintain his balance. "Are you ready to confess?"

"Yes."

"Then here, take my shoes. Put them on."

"No one's going to believe…" I began.

A slap filled the air. My face burned. Jordan pulled off the new shoes I'd recently purchased for him and put on the Northways. They were more than a little big.

"Tie them."

The shoes tied, Jordan looked at me. "I'm sorry, he said." I loved Audrey and I love you."

So, that was it, the real truth.

I thought about what Jordan had said about Chad and Janine fighting, but it didn't make sense. It made more sense that Jordan and Chad had been fighting about Audrey, or that Janine had a gripe with Jordan, than the first scenario. But then again, maybe Chad hadn't wanted to help Janine with the killing of Audrey Wilkins. What hold might she have had over him?

"Go!" Janine pushed us in front of her, and opening the door, shoved us outside. "Get in the car!"

I couldn't see a car, but Jordan walked around back and there it was waiting. It was an old thing, a Plymouth, and the tires were about as bald as the snow now fading on the mountain tops. The sky was dark, and I knew it would be nigh to impossible to get any attention as we drove from the school.

She pushed us inside, both of us in front, and locked the doors behind her." I don't want to hear anything from you!" she said, speeding from the school and driving up the main road. I remembered the time my mom had been kidnapped. I was suddenly remembering

185

lots of things I wished had been forgotten from my mind. But then, maybe it was good to remember. How had she escaped?

And then I remembered something else. My Mom hadn't made it out of the captive's car, and I wouldn't be leaving the car if I didn't do as I was told.

My body shivered and I thought about Jordan and how much I cared about him too, I heard something else. Something distinct. Something not unlike breathing.

Jordan was breathing heavily beside me. Though I tried to calm him with my hand, his body shuddered next to mine, and large tears were escaping his hazel eyes. "Shhh," I said as silently as I could. "Listen."

I wasn't sure if Jordan had heard it, and I hoped that Janine hadn't, but the breathing had been distinct only seconds before, breathing coming from the back seat.

I didn't dare look. I didn't dare do anything as Jordan and I lay huddled together. Except pray.

When the car stopped at the first light I took in a breath and waited.

Sure enough, long arms reached forward and slipped over Janine's neck. Letting go of Jordan I tumbled to the driver's side and reached for the brake, pushing down on it with my hands. The car swerved to the right. A car honked behind us, but I kept my hands riveted to the spot.

Janine gasped for air, her arms flailing to the sides, and above her, Conner's face peeked over the driver's seat. "Enough!" Conner yelled. "We're going to get out of this car and you're going to tell me what's going on!"

Conner semi-stood and reached for Janine's coat, holding her fast.

"I can't believe you're here!" Janine sang, as if all Conner had done was surprise her with a friendly visit.

"You're going to get out of the car and wait for me."

"Okay." The voice was quiet, and so unlike Janine I couldn't believe it. Where were the forceful words now? The brute strength she professed to have?

Janine opened the door and got out, Conner following behind, and as the two of them stood at the side of the road, all I could hear was garbled conversation.

"Are you okay?" I asked Jordan.

"Yes. You?"

"I'm fine. Let's sit up a bit." We were tall enough now to see through the windows. Conner and Janine were whispering outside of the car. I looked at Conner and then back at Jordan. His eyes were searching my own." I love you," he said again.

"I love you, too," I said, holding him close.

Jordan's breath was about as rancid as a sick cow but I didn't care. I really did love him. Not in the girlfriend/boyfriend way that I had once felt for Conner, but in a brother and sister way that I felt for Oscar, and I wanted Jordan to know it.

"You're like a brother to me."

Jordan took in a quick breath.

"Kiss me," he said.

Jordan reached for me, pulling my face closer. I could hear the voices outside; the noise level had increased. I wondered if the person behind us had decided to go around, or if they were watching the event like I was.

Conner and Janine were swathed in the darkness. All I could make out were their silhouettes.

"Kiss me, please!"

Jordan's voice had changed. It was almost as if he was begging or something. As I looked into his eyes I could see pain there, even in the darkness. He was holding me close. Almost too close. "We almost had you," he said. "Almost."

A coldness like steel touched my neck.

"Jordan?"

"Be still. Kiss me. Now."

I knew what was at my neck just as I knew the night was dark and that we were at the side of the road and that the car behind us was gone. Conner was here. He was outside speaking to Janine and I was inside the car with Jordan, and he was holding the scalpel to my neck.

Darkness

If I told you I was as afraid as I'd ever been, I'm sure you would believe me. But when I tell you what I did next, you might think I needed my head examined.

I kissed him.

It was the worst sensation in the world, but I did it. And then I told Jordan the biggest lie I'd ever told another living soul.

"I love you. I was too afraid to tell you before, but you need to know I love you."

I didn't see the scalpel, but a sudden emptiness caressed my neck. I knew the blade had been removed." I have loved you for a long time, but I didn't know you loved me back."

Jordan smiled, wiped at his tears and looked out. "We need to do something about Conner," he said. "He wasn't part of the plan."

"What plan?" I kissed Jordan one more time, taking in the sweat, the dirt, the awfulness of him, and took his hand.

"The plan to get you to love me."

"I guess it worked," I said, though my heart was beating from fear and not from love. I was sick inside. I really had loved him, though not in the way he'd wanted.

Looking past him as he held me, I searched for Conner. They were still talking, and the biggest part of me wanted him to notice that I was in trouble. But I couldn't scream. I couldn't do anything but pretend that we were all right.

"What do you want to do?" I asked.

"I have to know you no longer love him," Jordan said, pulling me away and looking into my eyes.

"I don't," I said, this time truthfully. Weeks before, when Jordan and I had searched for clues together, I had realized something about myself – something that had surprised me at first, but something that I was grateful I finally knew.

Jordan wiped away a tear I didn't even know was on my cheek. "You do love me," he said. "In a minute, we can tell them all."

"Janine doesn't know yet?"

"She knows, but I need to tell you the truth. Now that I know the truth about how you feel." He smiled tenderly at me, and it was all I could do not to jerk away from him. "She has been so patient with me. When I helped her with Audrey Wilkins I asked her if she could help me with you. She said she would be happy to."

My heart burned. "Who killed Audrey?"

"The girl I loved was the girl Janine hated. Imagine that. When Audrey broke it off with me for good, it was time for me to move on. With Janine's help, it was easy enough."

I leaned in and gave Jordan another kiss. This one was longer, and it was all I could do to remain calm.

"I told her I felt bad for killing someone I had loved but she told me that she'd get me an even better girl. And she was right. I have."

Jordan kissed me. Another tear slipped down my cheek. I couldn't believe it, any of it, but as Conner and Janine returned to the car, I sat still, waiting for a cue, anything that would tell me that Conner was somehow aware of the danger I was in.

***

I was told to get into the back seat with Jordan. I complied. Conner sat in the front next to Janine, his hand in hers. What had happened out there? What was he doing?

It occurred to me that maybe Conner was doing something similar to what I was doing and that maybe I should play along. Conner hadn't turned to me once, and the silence in the car was deafening. Finally, Janine spoke up. "I'm glad everything is settled. Are you two ok?"

"We're great!" Jordan sang. My mouth had opened to speak but Jordan had beaten me to it. I sat next to him, my hand within his, my heart wanting escape.

Conner turned around briefly from the front seat. He smiled at me, but his brown eyes weren't in it. They were cold, like glass." I have convinced Janine that it's time we go out on our first date. What do you think, guys, do you want to double?"

Jordan nodded. I followed suit – hoping, no praying – that the feelings now coursing through my veins were correct. Conner *was* doing what I was doing. And we were going to find a safe place to escape them both.

***

The pizza wasn't that good, but that may have been because my stomach was still sick. As I sat there next to Jordan and Conner sat next to Janine, I thought about how we would escape. Perhaps Conner was thinking the same thing; I occasionally saw his eyes leave Janine's face and travel to the door or window. And then they would return.

I did the same when I could, searching for a way out.

As far as I knew the scalpel had been put back in Jordan's pant pocket. As far as I knew there was no other weapon. As I ate, I'd occasionally take a look at Conner and I felt as if I could almost read his thoughts. He was

192

acting, too, and he was just as ready to escape as I was. Only, how?

There were plenty of people in the pizzeria on a Friday night, even more coming and going as we ate. I smiled as if on cue, and Conner told a joke or two, but it was all pretend, and my skin was having a hay day. I felt queasy all over, and every time the waitress came to our table I wanted to shout: "We've been kidnapped!"

But something kept me from yelling out. Something in Conner's eyes. He would work it out, and I would know it when the time came.

It happened when we were way into the dessert – a warm chocolate chip cookie layered with a scoop of vanilla ice cream and chocolate sauce. Conner dropped his spoon. It clanked to the floor and he bent down to retrieve it.

The table flew and I suddenly realized that Conner had gone beneath it, lifting the thing with his body and pushing it off the floor.

I was quickly out the door without looking back. Only when I'd reached the parking lot did I stop. Connor was wrestling Jordan to the floor and Janine was screaming, pounding on Conner's back. People were standing now. Some were staring, others were leaving the restaurant. Though it was more than likely shut, I could hear all the noise through the door and windows. I knew Connor was strong, stronger than Jordan at least. I prayed he was also stronger than Janine. Still, he must have known her limits, discovered them through the years they'd been friends.

In a moment, Conner, too, would free himself from danger.

Only, he never came.

I waited. I'd left my purse in the restaurant so I couldn't check my phone. I waited in the cold as people came out, some shaking their heads, others seemingly oblivious to what was happening inside. One of the patrons approached me.

I was standing behind a van and the patron's car was parked opposite. "I'd go if I were you," the man said, whisking his wife into the front seat and shutting the door. He turned to me once more before getting inside. "Someone's been hurt."

But I didn't leave. I hid behind the van until the police arrived. I watched as they brought out Jordan and then Janine from within. I watched Conner's face as they asked him questions. I saw him look in my direction, hoping to see me I suppose. But I didn't move from behind the van until the owners finally came to reclaim it.

"It's safe now," they said, but it was hard for me to believe it. I had gone for years and years without being terribly afraid. I'd had bad times with my first parents, had fought with Conner, had even seen a dead girl in the park, but nothing held a candle to what I'd experienced the last few hours.

I felt as if, somehow, I'd been sliced open, and everyone from then on would see all of my innards – all of my guts. I felt dissected and I didn't like it.

I was about a half-an-hour's walk from home. It was dark, cold and I couldn't get the chills to escape my body. I couldn't believe I was alive. I couldn't believe any of it.

***

Dad held me. He was shaking. Mom held my hand, stroking it like a small puppy. I couldn't believe my heart. It wasn't working right. Oscar was in the room, too, and so was Conner. The police were long gone, at least for a while, and all I could think about was how naked I felt.

It was a strange feeling, something I don't think I can explain to you, but I felt so lonely and so afraid for the first time. Jordan and Janine were in jail. The scalpel was in police custody. The story – at least my side of it, and the side of Conner and my parents – had been told.

I'd also been told by Conner that Jordan had shrieked about Audrey in the last moments as they fought on the floor and that the blood coming from Jordan's leg had been his own fault, for keeping such a dangerous weapon in his pocket.

But I didn't want to think about it anymore. I didn't want to think about Audrey lying dead at Montgomery Park, her hair spread out like the sun by

Jordan's dirty hands. I didn't want to think about the keychain, left there long after the murder by Jordan because he'd started to fall for me and wanted to bury the past. I didn't want to think about Janine carrying Audrey's body from the car, and before that, from the makeshift home of Jordan Elspie – where she and Jordan had met before her last breath. Audrey's blood would eventually be found hidden underneath the door mat, but now it was all about breathing in and out – in and out.

Later, it would be discovered that Jordan's father was still alive. That he'd been out drinking the night I'd come to save Jordan, someone who didn't need saving, at least not in the way I'd been thinking at the time. I learned that the police had been uncertain of the killer until I'd come to them with news of the Northway shoes. They'd watched me after that, and, when the call came from the restaurant, it was Officer Hybrid who had run in first looking for me.

No one could calm me, not even my dad. He tried though, and we had many talks the next few days before his passing. I'm not sure if I believed he was gone even then, but I knew that I loved him more than anyone else in the world other than Mom and even Oscar.

"I know you'll be a great detective," he said that last night before I left his room, never to speak with him again. "Look what you've done with Audrey Wilkins. Imagine how relieved her parents are to know who took the life of their daughter."

"But for what – jealousy?"

"Crimes of passion, they're all the rage," he'd said then, bringing me in close. Since the word that I was safe, my dad's health had gone downhill. It was no surprise that he'd gotten ill after I returned home; I knew he'd been worried and all that, but a person doesn't really think of their father dying, even when all of the signs are there.

Dad held me for long time and we spoke about the adoption, my life now as compared to the past. But mostly we spoke about my desires for the future. In a strange way, it was if my dad knew he was going to go and he wanted to be sure I had my head on straight.

Mom joined us and then Oscar, sitting on the side of the bed, peering at Father from a distance. I don't know if he ever got close, though I'm sure Mom did. I left them and went back to my room, dreaming of my life here, a safe place that I still managed to add some intrigue to, if not in my room directly or my home, then in the life I'd created for myself when it came to sleuthing.

Searching for the killer of Audrey Wilkins had been difficult, but it had been rewarding, too, and I figured I'd be searching for the truth for a long time. I wasn't sure what would come for me in the future, but I hoped it was good.

When the court day came and went I discovered that Chad had had nothing to do with the events that had unfolded with Audrey Wilkins. He'd been nothing but a plant for me, so that I wouldn't see who the killer really was. Even my friendship with Jordan and his words about Conner had been given to me so that my focus would be on him instead of the real culprits of the crime. Sure, Conner had had some problems in the past, while he lived in Jersey, but unbeknownst to me he'd been in therapy in Utah. He hadn't wielded anything but his anger in quite a while.

I knew I didn't really love Conner, not because he got angry sometimes or anything like that, but because I'd been looking for love in all the wrong places. I know saying that sounds a bit cliché but sometimes we look for things we think will make us happy, only to discover the real truth – albeit a hard one – that truth can only come from seeing things as they really are.

With Conner, it had always been about how he smelled, like mint aftershave, his dark brown eyes looking into my own, and feeling loved by him, even when things got awkward and I wondered what I was really doing with him.

When I talked to his sister about my feelings, she apologized to me for coming to my house that night and freaking me out about him. "We yell a lot here," she said, as if that made all the difference, and that somehow, I would change my mind about breaking up with him. He actually loved me it seemed, at least that's how it felt as we hugged for the last time and he told me that his feelings for me had always been genuine. He would work on his anger, he said. Maybe later, when he was more solid, we could date again.

I'd recently gone to visit Carol, Audrey's mom, at *Clarities*, and we'd actually been able to talk about her and the feelings Audrey had had for Jordan. Evidently, she hadn't loved Jordan in the same way that he'd professed to love her either, and it had caused some friction – and eventually her death.

It was funny, but despite everything, I still felt that sisterly sort of love for Jordan, though I realized that, had I not acted in the way I had, I would have more than likely been Jordan's next victim. I felt sorry for Audrey, kind-hearted though she was, and wanted to hate Jordan for being so messed-up that he thought the only solution came from using the sharp end of a scalpel.

But I couldn't hate him.

"I had no idea it had gotten so bad. If I'd only known," Carol said.

I couldn't blame her. I hadn't known either, how bad 'professed' love could really get. How like a lie it could turn out to be.

Carol had cried then, and I'd wiped at my own tears. I missed my dad. I missed his funny ways and how calm he was even during the last hours. It had never been about him. It had always been about us: Mom, Oscar and I.

And that was something I would never forget.

TIE DIED

www.ingramcontent.com/pod-product-compliance
Lightning Source LLC
Chambersburg PA
CBHW070749180626
46818CB00007B/3044